The Shaman's Secret ❧

Natasha Narayan █████ England at the a██ ██ ████ journalism includ█ ██ in Bosnia. Like K███ places. Visiting th█ ████ ██████ exciting experiences of her childhood.

∾ The Kit Salter Adventures by Natasha Narayan ∾

❧ A Kit Salter Adventure ❧

The Shaman's Secret

❧ Natasha Narayan ❧

Quercus

First published in Great Britain in 2011 by

Quercus
21 Bloomsbury Square
London
WC1A 2NS

A CIP catalogue reference for this book is available
from the British Library

ISBN 978 1 84916 555 6

1 3 5 7 9 10 8 6 4 2

Designed and typeset by Nigel Hazle
Printed and bound in Great Britain by Clays Ltd, St Ives plc.

For my friend Nina,
❧ who set up her own orphanage: ☙
www.milliemittoochildrensprojects.com

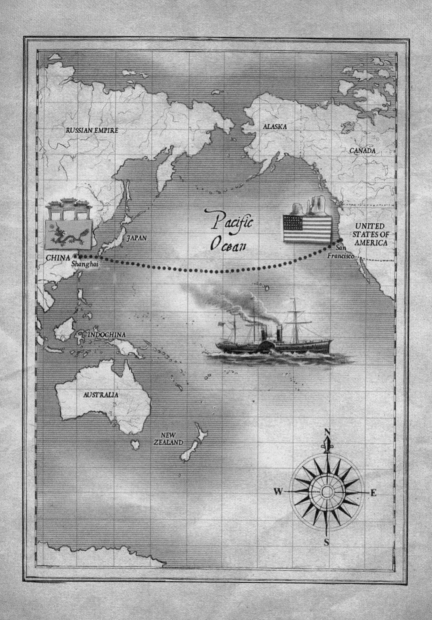

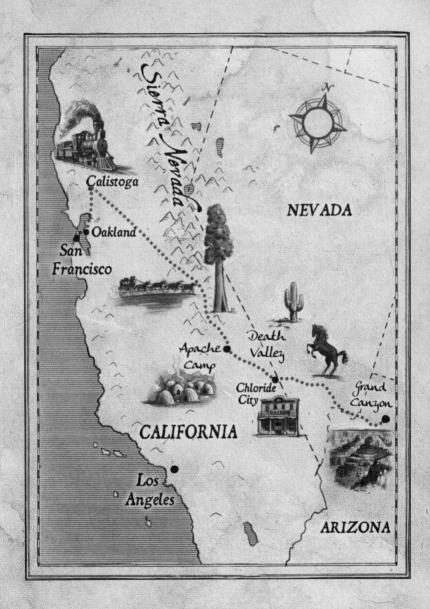

❧ Chapter One ❧

Waldo Bell's Story
San Francisco, 1878

'Come on, Waldo,' Isaac whispered as I bent down to blow out the candles on the birthday cake. 'Big puff. For Kit's sake.'

Thirteen candles stood on the cake, thirteen wisps of flame. One for each year of Kit Salter's life.

'Not so fast,' a voice boomed in my ear. I felt Kit's Aunt Hilda tugging at my shirt. 'I've changed my mind.'

'What are you—'

'Stand down.' She elbowed me aside, her face full of dogged determination. 'Kit would have wanted a girl to do this.'

'You're hardly a girl . . .' Rachel blurted, then stopped, reddening.

Hilda glared at her. 'A woman, at any rate. Besides, I'm family.'

I moved out of the way. Only a madman would try to

1

stop Hilda Salter when she was in full flow. She stood in the boarding-house parlour, glowering at that harmless cake as if it was the enemy. There was no obvious reason for her anger. A beautiful creation, the Madeira sponge rose in white tiers with a marzipan figure of Kit Salter on top. Aunt Hilda leaned over and, with a single puff from her bulldog lungs, the candles went out.

I felt sorry, somehow, to see them vanish so fast.

We were celebrating Kit's thirteenth birthday party in our boarding house in San Francisco. Everything *was* perfect. The presents, the silver vats of punch, the mountains of scones and buns. Everything was just fine, but never had a birthday party felt so much like a funeral. Kit sat by the fire in her bath chair, a blanket over her knees. It was sunny outside, the buds bursting from the California orange trees and the birds in full song. Yet the doctor had ordered that Kit must have fire and blankets at all times.

It was all wrong. You know how Kit is, blazing with energy, jabbering non-stop. Now she just lay in bed night and day, her face empty. She needed a nurse to wash and feed her. Her eyes stared at nothing and she moved not an inch. We could have been pouring out our congratulations to a china doll.

Kit had been in a coma for over six months, since we'd left China. She had not said one word – which, I'm sure you're aware, is highly unusual – not so much as a blink or a stir or a sneeze. Our adventures, which had taken us from the deserts of Egypt to the frozen peaks of the Himalayas, had been cruelly cut short.

So why bother having a party for her? you may well ask. In part it was to cheer *us* up. Rachel and her brother, Isaac; her aunt, Hilda Salter; and I, Waldo Bell, had all spent six months in hell. We were on tenterhooks, hoping every morning that *this* would be the day. This would be the special day Kit would sit up and surprise us all by ordering breakfast.

It hadn't happened, not so far.

But there was another more important reason why we were holding the birthday tea.

The doctor on the ship back from China had told me to treat Kit as if she understood what we were saying. 'Just talk,' he'd said. 'You never know what might go in.' So I sat and rambled on. I poured secrets out to her, which I would never have told the waking Kit. Other times, I didn't quite know where my thoughts ended and my words began.

Sometimes I would get angry with Kit for being so damned obstinate and with myself for letting her take stupid, unnecessary risks in China. The risks that had landed her in a coma.

But I'm becoming gloomy. This was a happy day, Kit's birthday, a time to smile and put on a brave face. No use dwelling on these wasted months in San Francisco, trudging from doctor to doctor, seeking anyone who could cure Kit. We had even gone to witch doctors and spiritualists, to the craziest healers out there.

Not one made a jot of difference.

No wonder. This coma, which had struck her down in China when she had held the bones of a long-dead saint, was beyond the understanding of science.

'Before we cut the cake, let's all have a sing-song,' Rachel suggested, going to the piano. 'Kit loves music.'

'No, she doesn't,' Kit's aunt said. 'She couldn't hold a tune to save her life.'

'It doesn't do to speak ill of the –' Rachel stopped mid-sentence.

'Out with it, Rebecca! DEAD. D.E.A.D. My niece is not dead. She is merely asleep and any day now she WILL wake up. I, Hilda Salter, demand it.'

'I didn't mean "dead".' Rachel was flustered, her brown hair falling all over her face. 'I didn't mean "dead".' Her voice was rising hysterically.

Isaac, meanwhile, was sitting in an armchair next to the comatose Kit. I don't think he heard a word, for his gaze was fixed on the cake. He hadn't done anything but gaze hungrily at that cake since he'd entered the room.

'Let's have some cake,' he suggested. 'Kit prefers cake to music.'

'Good idea,' Hilda grunted. Picking up the silver slicer,

she cut herself a generous wodge and tucked in. 'Well, Rebecca, I dare say I've tasted worse,' she said to Rachel, who had spent hours slaving over that cake. 'I'm beginning to see what you're *for*.'

Just then there came a knock at the parlour door. In came Bessie the maid.

'There's a gentleman outside, asking for you, madam,' she said to Aunt Hilda.

'Show him in. I suppose we have enough cake to go round,' Aunt Hilda ordered.

I was going to protest, because it seemed rude to Kit to spoil her party, but Bessie had disappeared. In a few minutes the oddest-looking gentleman in San Francisco stood in our parlour. He was obviously English, for he was dressed in a good-quality top hat and frock coat that had come from one of London's better tailors. He had ruddy cheeks, long wispy hair that stuck out below his hat and a bulbous pink nose that showed him to be a serious drinker. His eyes darted around the parlour as if valuing the contents.

I took an instant dislike to the man – he gave off the odour of some cheap huckster. I was willing to bet he was all set to try to sell us something.

'Well, get on with it, man,' Aunt Hilda snapped. 'You're interrupting a private party.'

'I beg leave to present my credentials,' he said, offering a thick cream envelope to Aunt Hilda.

Aunt Hilda opened the envelope and drew out a piece of paper. I sidled over to her and read:

Professor Dr Walter Silas, Phd, MD, FRS, mmd, doclit, LLD, dip eng

Expert in curing incurable conditions

Are you in despair?
Fear not, Dr Silas is here!

Dr Silas has had incredible results with all types of tics, nerve troubles, comas and hysteric and mental conditions.

> 'He raised my Georgie from the dead.'
> *Patricia Lupone, mother of George, 11*

> 'Medical science seemed to have abandoned us. We thought all hope was gone till we put our trust in Dr Silas.'
> *Helen Smith, whose husband Althelred*
> *was raised from an 'incurable' coma*

Dr Silas's patented galvanic electro-shake machine has had outstanding results. Try it on your loved ones – he can bring new life to dead bones!

'Are you Dr Silas?' Hilda asked him.

'No, madam. I'm Harold Rumbelow, his humble servant.'

'How on earth do you know my niece is unwell? I take it that's why you're here.'

The man made a sweeping bow so low his nose nearly touched his heaving belly.

'We have heard it on the grapevine, your ladyship.'

'I have not been ennobled – yet,' Aunt Hilda said stiffly. 'Anyway, what grapevine?'

'Your niece's plight, as you visited every reputable doctor – and, I beg your pardon, scandalous quack – has come to my master's attention. He acts from the purest motives, naturally.'

The man cut a seedy figure. He did not inspire trust. But we were at our wits' end. We had to help Kit; anything was better than nothing.

Aunt Hilda scanned the letter: 'How does this so-called galvanic electro-shake contraption work?' she asked.

'The mysteries of electricity,' replied the man, bowing again. 'I do not understand it myself, but my master . . . Well, ladies and gents, I do not boast when I tell you that he has, literally, worked miracles.'

Isaac watched him thoughtfully. 'They've had some remarkable results with electricity,' he said. 'Thinking it over, I can see that a good shock might be just what the nervous system needs to stimulate it into renewed activity.'

'Eh?' I asked, looking at him in puzzlement.

'It may work. Waldo, Hilda, I think we should give it a try.'

Rachel bit her lip and said, in a trembling little voice, 'I agree with my brother. I mean, what have we to lose?'

Aunt Hilda turned to the fellow and said, 'Thank your master for coming to our aid, my good man. We may well consult him. But we cannot take such a giant step till Professor Salter, my brother, has arrived. You may take a piece of cake as you leave.'

He was being dismissed, but the man stood there looking obstinate.

'Madam, pardon me saying this, but I think you should come tomorrow. My master said time is of the essence.'

Aunt Hilda flushed deep red. 'How dare you? If we seek to consult you, we will do it when we see fit. Now, off you go. Go on. Goodbye.'

There was nothing more the man could say. Bowing again and casting a mournful look at the cake, he backed out of the door. He never did get his slice.

'That was strange,' I said, looking after him.

'Strange? How so?' Isaac asked.

'I mean that he should come and visit us and be in quite

such a hurry that Kit has treatment with his master. It seems rather suspicious to me.'

'This is a small city. I am something of a legend in these parts,' Aunt Hilda said, dismissing my concerns with a wave of her podgy hands. 'Tomorrow you will look for my dratted brother again. I am keen to start on this treatment as soon as possible.'

She might have waved away my fears, but something still struck me as odd about that little red-nosed man.

❧ Chapter Two ❧

After breakfast, I started on my mission to find out what had happened to Kit's father. I was glad to be away from the poky boarding house. To be honest, Isaac, Aunt Hilda and even kind Rachel were grating on my nerves. I strode up Sacramento Street, past the buildings that my fellow Americans had put up on the back of gold-rush fever. San Francisco is a miracle city. Just fifty years ago it was a scrubby wasteland. Look at it now. Surrounded by hills, the Pacific Ocean at its feet, thronged with gracious streets. Pines, mimosa and scarlet hibiscus bloom in the parks. It proves that anything Britain can do America can do bigger and better. The mansions of the millionaire 'robber barons' on Nob Hill are the finest in the world.

I was proud to be an American in Frisco. Proud to be young, strong and free to make my fortune. Yet somehow today I couldn't enjoy the city. I'd planned to catch a cab to the telegraph office, but once out I just kept walking and walking.

My feet hit the pavement savagely. The exercise was

what I needed to keep the blood from beating in my head. God, was I angry. I felt like kicking something. I pounded the streets so furiously that I made it to the Western Union telegraph office in under half an hour.

I begged the clerk at the counter for messages from Professor Salter. Unfortunately there was nothing from the old gentleman, no news at all. Sighing, I turned away. I would have to check all the hotels and boarding houses, *again*.

I was just about to leave the office when I heard a familiar bleating voice.

'Is there really nothing you can do?' a gentleman in a shabby black coat and a stovepipe hat was asking another clerk.

'I'm sorry, sir, but you have no address,' the clerk said.

'It's desperately important, you see. My daughter's ill.'

'We have your details on file.'

I strode up to the man. At the risk of real rudeness if it was the wrong person, I swung him round by the shoulder. To my relief Professor Salter was drooping in front of me.

'Isaac, my dear fellow,' he gasped.

'I'm Waldo,' I said. 'Waldo Bell.'

'Of course, Waldo. How glad I am to see you.'

'And I you, sir. What happened to you? We've been expecting you for a month or more.'

He flushed. 'I'm afraid I lost your letters.'

'Lost our letters?'

'I've been at my wit's end. Trying all the hotels, the docks, the office here.'

'We weren't at a hotel. We're staying at Isaac Hilton's Temperance hostel. It was the only place with rooms available when we arrived. Shall we go back there now? You must be anxious to see Kit.'

'Of course, my dear fellow,' said Professor Salter, looking up the street to where a cab was hurtling by. 'But I should pick up my luggage first.'

'If you like. Where are you staying?'

'Pardon me?'

I sighed. 'Where are you living, Professor Salter?'

Professor Salter flushed again. 'Ah yes,' he said. 'I will take you there.'

I followed him as he wound his way through the back alleys. Sometimes, though I knew the professor to be extremely clever, he was as simple as a baby. I could see what Kit meant when she referred to herself as her father's nursemaid.

Eventually we arrived at his boarding house, which turned out to be a shabby building in the wrong part of town. I stared at it in dismay. One of the windows was boarded up, and when we entered there was a strong smell of cabbage and grease. No wonder I hadn't found the professor when I'd combed the streets. I had forgotten how thrifty he could be with his money. He wouldn't spend a penny on himself if he didn't have to. With Kit, of course, he was very generous. Nothing was too good for her.

We were let in by a dumpy Irish lady with a sharp tongue, who smelt of stew. She scolded the professor as he led me up to his room. It was in chaos, with books and papers everywhere. It turned out he had been living here, looking for us, for more than a month.

What a mess.

I had to rescue him. I asked the professor to pack an overnight bag. The other possessions I would arrange to have picked up later. Then I went down to pay the landlady, who was very disagreeable. When I went back upstairs I found Kit's father had made no progress in packing. He was sitting in the room's single shabby armchair, staring into space.

'Professor Salter,' I said gently, 'we should hurry. Kit is waiting to see you.'

She wasn't, in reality. But I had to urge him from his daydream.

'Must hurry. Quite right, dear boy,' he said. But he didn't move, just continued to stare into space.

'May I help?' I asked, moving over and placing a hand on his arm.

He shrank back into his seat.

'Professor. Please. What is it?'

He didn't reply. For a moment, I think, he had forgotten I was there. I bit back my frustration. At this moment the good professor was behaving as if it was he, not his poor daughter, who was in a coma. I knew, deep down, that there was nothing I could do to hurry him up. Kit's father is a dreamy old dear; he lives in his own world. For his daughter's sake I had to respect that, and not try to rush him into normal behaviour. So I sat on the dusty floorboards by his armchair and waited.

When I next looked up, because I had fallen into a bit of a daze myself, I saw tears in his eyes.

'Theo,' I said, using his first name. 'Please, what is the matter?'

He looked at me. 'It's no good. I can't do it.'

'Can't do what?'

'I can't come back to your hotel.'

'Why ever not?'

A tear slipped out of his left eye and rolled down his cheek, coming to rest in his grizzled beard.

'I just can't.'

'Why? Surely you want to see Kit as soon as possible.'

'I – can't.'

I stared at him, horrified.

'You don't understand anything. You're just a boy. You see, I saw Tabby die. I can't –' He broke off.

'What is Tabby?' I asked, thinking it might be the name of a favourite cat.

In answer he reached into his pocket and drew out a fine gold chain. Hanging from it was a small locket. I opened it and the likeness of a lovely young woman gazed out at me. She had an oval face, unruly springing hair and eyes that even in that tiny miniature flashed with fire. Instantly I knew who it was. The likeness was unmistakable. Kit's mother.

'My wife, Tabitha. She was brought to me that December night. Ten inches of snow we'd had. A white Christmas, the church bells ringing. Her pelvis had been fractured. Her nose crushed. They said it was an accident. A startled dray horse. She lay in the bed. Looked at me, her eyes always so bright. But, you see, they were all that was left of her. Her eyes. All the rest was blood and –'

His voice broke into gasps and he stopped, looking down at his shoes. I put an arm round his shoulders. What could I say? I felt awkward, because he was the father . . . Well, let's just say I felt strange embracing him. There was a lump in my own throat, which hurt like hell.

'I saw Tabby die,' he said. 'It wasn't good or peaceful. Anyone who tells you that is lying. I can't watch the same thing with—'

'Kit is not going to die,' I said. 'You must believe me. We will save her.

15

'I can't see her in pain.'

'She is not in pain. The doctor assures us of that.'

He looked at me as if I was lying to him, his eyes blurred with tears.

'Professor. You must come. She loves you.'

He shook his head.

'You're her *father*. She *needs* you.'

He rocked back, as if I had struck him.

'It is your duty,' I said, though I felt my words were cruel. 'Please come. You will never forgive yourself if you don't.'

'Very well,' he said. Heavily he pulled himself out of the armchair, moving like a very old man. As I watched, he placed a pair of socks into his Gladstone bag.

❧ Chapter Three ❧

Professor Salter looked up from his daughter's bed and stared at me. His mood had changed as he came into the bedroom. The tears were gone; in their place was a simmering anger.

'What did you do to her?' he asked.

'I haven't done—'

'Kit was well when I last saw her. My lovely girl . . . and now I find her like this. You were the only person there when she was struck down. You were meant to be protecting her.'

I nodded. Kit was lying there between us, white and thin. She looked waxy, like a corpse. He was right. I should have looked after her better.

'You're not a boy. You're a young man. Older than my daughter . . .'

'I'm sorry,' I mumbled. I felt choked, and for a horrible moment I thought I would cry. Kit was covered with one of those American patchwork quilts, the bright colours contrasting with her waxy bluish skin. 'Professor Salter . . .'

17

I began, but Aunt Hilda shushed me and took her brother's arm.

'It's not Waldo's fault,' she said.

'I read your letters. You told me about it,' he said, turning on her. 'You said that Waldo was the only one in the cave . . . Why did he take her there in the first place? A young, innocent girl. That's what I want to know. What did you think you were playing at, young man?' Anger had mottled the professor's skin and bright red patches stood out on his cheeks. 'My dearest Kit . . .' His voice broke.

'Theo,' Aunt Hilda tried to soothe him.

'I should horsewhip you!' He glared at me, trembling.

'Yes, sir.' I hung my head.

My answer seemed to take the puff out of him. He collapsed into an armchair and covered his face with his hands. There were shabby patches on his jacket. Patches Kit would have taken care of.

'I would do anything . . . anything,' I said quietly, 'never to have set foot in that blasted—'

'Enough,' Professor Salter interrupted. His mood had changed again; his eyes had become hard. He turned to his sister, Hilda. 'The question is, what are we going to do?'

Hilda hesitated for a few seconds before replying. 'Of course Kit has seen doctors here, the best doctors that money—'

18

'Doctors!' Professor Salter threw up his arms. 'What do doctors know?'

'Theo. You are a man of science.'

'They didn't help Tabby,' he snapped. For a moment brother and sister glared at each other.

'Tabby was an accident, Theo.'

'*That's what they said.* And now Kit – doesn't that strike you as strange?'

'Look, Theo, there is something else we could try.' Aunt Hilda dived into her pocket and produced the leaflet that the man had pressed on us last night. Theo smoothed it out and read it. Several times. I could see he was struggling to understand what it meant. Grief had dulled his wits.

'What is this?' he said at last.

'I've asked around,' Aunt Hilda replied. 'This man, Walter Silas, he is well thought of in San Francisco. Apparently he has worked miracle cures on many hopeless cases.'

'Sounds like a fraud,' Professor Salter said, looking at the leaflet again. 'Is there any evidence for this?'

'We're desperate. What have we to lose?'

'So you want to use my Kit, my . . .' He paused, glaring at both of us. 'You want to *experiment* on her. You really think that's a clever idea?'

We looked back at him in silence.

The next morning, the five of us went through the back of a large grey stone building into a garden that ended in a tumbledown shed. Here among coils of wire, bolts, nails and strange contraptions sat a man who could have been the double of Professor Salter. Walter Silas was wiry and untidy, with a shock of grey hair and protruding eyes. Perfectly friendly, but one of those people you feel is *not listening* most of the time.

'He's away with the fairies,' Aunt Hilda whispered to me as we sat on a dirty wooden bench. 'Waldo, I'm nervous.'

I gripped her arm for a second. Frankly I was scared out of my wits.

We had argued for hours last night about bringing Kit to Professor Silas's workshop. Finally we had all agreed it was the right thing to do. It was a chance, however slim. The alternative was that Kit could lie in a coma for years. Her life would be wasted.

I think Professor Salter cheered up a little when he saw the workshop. Like Isaac, he is a man of science, and was in his element here. And I think, for our clever friend Isaac, this grubby shed was heaven. He picked everything up and examined it and by the time the helmet was ready to go on Kit's head he had elbowed out the cloddish Rumbelow and was acting as Silas's assistant.

As Kit lay corpse-like on a stretcher, dressed in a lacy white cotton nightgown, Isaac fiddled with the bolts

20

on a shining copper helmet. We were going to put this dangerous new substance, electricity, through my friend's delicate brain. This could kill Kit; that's what I thought as I watched Silas fiddle with his machine. It could kill her stone dead.

The galvanic electro-shake was a curious contraption, about the size of a small man, made of copper with dozens of knobs down the front, like the buttons on a shirt. Wires sprayed out of it, blue, red and green. Kit was laid on a table and covered in a sheet, her head encased in a copper helmet, which was taken off the machine. Wires ran to her splayed fingers. I didn't understand what these scientists planned to do – I won't pretend to you that I did.

Finally all the preparations were finished and the machine was switched on.

'Wait,' I called, just before they were about to start the electrical stimulation. I looked straight at Mr Silas. 'Have you ever conducted an experiment like this before, sir?'

'Of course,' Mr Silas replied airily. 'I'm a pioneer.'

'That suggests that this is the first time. Tell me, sir, how many patients have you tested the galvanic electro-shake on?'

'A dozen or so. At least, one or two or three. Can't remember exactly. Remarkable results in comatose cases and so on . . .'

'Lord help us,' Hilda Salter muttered under her breath.

'I usually work on bridges. These new cable cars – I told Isaac here about them. We'll go for a ride after this experiment.'

'No, we won't,' Hilda barked. 'Not unless . . .' and she stopped.

Rachel finished the sentence for her. 'I think, Mr Silas, none of us will want to go for a ride in a cable car. Not unless our friend Kit can come with us.'

Mr Silas flushed as he was reminded what his 'experiment' consisted of. 'Of course,' he said. 'I understand. Do I have your permission to proceed?'

Professor Salter nodded. His skin was grey, and there were deep rings under his eyes.

Without further ado, Mr Silas turned a knob on his contraption and, as we watched, a huge current travelled up the wires to Kit's head.

Nothing happened. Nothing.

I pulled my eyes away from Kit's white-sheeted body and looked around restlessly. I couldn't bear to see what was going on. At the door to the shed a figure in a cream linen suit had appeared. It was a man, who stood there watching. Something about the narrowness of his body, the stoop of his shoulders, was familiar. And the pale, pale skin.

But this man had black hair. Jet-black hair that contrasted oddly with his corpse-like pallor. A caterpillar-sized moustache curled above his upper lip.

It took me a few moments to recognise the man. It was Cecil Baker, our old enemy. Or was it his brother, Cyril? Both of them were murderers, monsters who wanted Kit dead. It only took me a moment, looking at him, to realise what he was doing here.

We had been tricked. This was a trap.

I turned to my friends, my mouth opening in an agonised yell.

Dr Silas said, 'Looks like we need more power.' He reached out and turned the middle red knob on his machine to maximum.

'STOP!' I shouted, launching myself towards the machine. 'FOR HEAVEN'S SAKE, STOP HIM! THEY ARE GOING TO KILL HER!'

Too late. A massive charge of electricity sizzled down those wires towards Kit's brain.

❧ Chapter Four ❧

Kit's Story

What am I doing here? One minute I am in China, in the caves above the Shaolin monastery. I am standing there, water dripping all around me, with the bones of a long-dead saint in my hands. The next minute I am waking in a shed full of twisted metal and wires . . . They tell me I am in America.

America, the new world.

My father, Isaac and Rachel. Their faces loomed above me as I lay on the table. My joints ached, the light hurt my eyes and my mouth felt dry. I tried to talk. My tongue was swollen. It felt unfamiliar, scaly, like a cobra coiled in my mouth.

'Kit?' Rachel was holding my hand, gulping. My father beside her, blocking out the light. He had aged, his hair a shocking white, new lines on his face. His eyes were wet. It made me feel strange. I had never seen Father cry before.

'I'll never leave you again. I promise,' Father muttered.

24

You didn't leave me, I wanted to say. *It was my fault, Father.* My tongue wouldn't work so I could only look at him and hope he knew what I meant. He held out his hand and took mine. My heart tumbled inside my chest. His image flickered and for a moment all I saw was his outline, muzzy, whitish against a glowing light.

'Don't punish me, Kit. I mean to spend much less time on my work. I *will* be a better father to you.'

What was he talking about? He is a wonderful father. Kind, generous and not too attentive to what I get up to.

Rachel was crying, fat tears dripping down her face. She let out a sob and used a tissue to blow her nose. Even Isaac's eyes were welling up. I couldn't cry. I felt a deep bewilderment. The world seemed soft, insubstantial, as I looked out at it. I remembered the feeling so strongly I could touch it, of peace, of being curled up in a deep, dark place.

A safe place.

'We must take her home,' Father said, turning to Rachel. 'We must take Kit back to Oxford as soon as possible.'

In the background I could hear shouting, screaming. It was somewhere far away, tinny to my ears. Something crashed and then clanged and clattered away across the floor. I could hear Waldo yelling and Aunt Hilda's deep voice. And someone else, someone whose voice was a high-pitched, ghastly whine.

25

Making a supreme effort, I pulled my body up. My ribs hurt and the breath came hard. Rachel and Isaac both rushed to stop me.

'Nooooo. You mustn't,' Rachel wailed. 'It is too soon.'

I had to. I had to *see*. I had managed to lever myself upright. Waldo and Aunt Hilda were bunched together, both talking at once. In front of them was a man – it came to me in a rush, Cecil Baker. No, not Cecil, his brother, Cyril. They were so alike it was hard to tell which of the twins it was. Or at least they used to be. This man was transformed. With hair dyed black, trimmed moustache. He looked more wrong than ever, like a ghost pretending to be a dandy.

'You don't understand,' Cyril said, his voice rising. 'It was me – I SAVED KIT'S LIFE.'

Waldo and Aunt Hilda both began shouting at once. Their voices rose hysterically. I heard the word 'killer' and 'get out'. A bookshelf full of screws and bolts had been overturned, and pieces of metal rolled all over the floor.

'YOU SHOULD BE THANKING ME, NOT CURSING ME,' Cyril Baker shouted.

You can make yourself do anything, even if your body rebels. My body was telling me to lie down and let all this pass, but I made up my own mind. Using all my strength, I sat up straight and spoke.

'YOU . . . SHOULD . . .'

26

Everyone in the shed stopped arguing and screaming and turned to me. There was pin-drop silence. I took a gulp of air, which streamed into my lungs, giving me new strength.

'LISTEN . . . TO . . . HIM.'

Having spoken, I collapsed back onto the table. Someone had propped a bolster behind me, so now I was sitting half upright. Five words, but they had a sensational effect. My friends looked astonished, as if a ghost had spoken, while Mr Baker's mouth widened in a broad smile.

'Kit Salter is finally back,' he said. 'You have me to thank for that.'

'Stand aside, you monster,' Aunt Hilda said to Mr Baker. To me she muttered, 'I'm so pleased to see you here again, my darling.' She glared at Mr Baker and then came over to enfold me in her stumpy arms. I struggled for a second and then relaxed into the embrace. She smoothed back a strand of hair and looked into my eyes.

'Welcome back, Kit,' she said, and then switched her attention to Baker. 'We all know that you hate my niece. We all know that she is the only one, apart from me, who has ever thwarted your plans.'

'I've changed,' Baker said. 'Ask Professor Silas.'

The shabby man he pointed to was cleaning a metal mannequin. He was bent over almost double, rubbing it with a soft cloth. As he worked, he clucked to himself.

Absorbed in his task, he hadn't heard Baker and didn't reply.

'Silas,' Baker called out, 'who sent you Rumbelow? Who funded your galvanic electro-shock machine? Didn't I make you seek out Kit Salter and cure her?'

'Perfectly true,' Silas replied. 'Why? Does it matter?'

'Of course it matters!' Aunt Hilda exploded. 'This man is our sworn enemy. He is a liar, a cheat and a murderer.'

'A murderer?' Silas asked.

'I know of at least five murders he has personally ordered.'

'No! Really? Are you sure?' Silas said. 'I mean, he's always been good to me. Paid in advance. Dollars. Nuggets of gold. Most generous terms.'

'He is rich,' Waldo said. 'But his wealth is based on death, slavery and—'

'Waldo,' I interrupted from my slumped position, 'let Baker talk. There is something . . . He may be telling the truth. Please—'

But Waldo and my aunt interrupted me indignantly, leaving me unable to finish.

Thankfully my father came to my aid. His angry voice sliced through the babble. 'NO ONE IS DOING ANY TALKING!' he said. 'We are going to take Kit home. She will rest. She will see a doctor. This is not the time for argument.'

He glared at the five of them: Waldo, Isaac, Rachel, my aunt and Baker. Shamefaced, my friends came forward and eased me onto the stretcher that lay near the table. Swaying between them, I was carried out into the garden. The last thing I saw was Mr Baker's pale face and black hair, looming over me like a deathless vampire.

❧ Chapter Five ❧

Over the next few days I was cocooned in gossamer, coddled like the weakest newborn babe. I was swaddled in soft blankets despite the heat, talked to in hushed voices. Nothing was too good for me. No food that I demanded too exotic. I was drowning in kindness.

I basked in the treatment, feeling strength return to my limbs and some clarity to my thoughts. *Some.* I confess I was still fuzzy, the colours of the world murky. I felt as if I had woken up after a long time in the deep sea and now saw the world through watery eyes.

By the fifth day, after the doctor had pronounced me miraculously better, I was getting a little tired of my hush-hush treatment.

'Aunt Hilda,' I said as the doctor was ushered out of the boarding-house parlour, 'I think we should see Cyril Baker.'

'That man? He already infests the place far too much.'

'What do you mean?'

'He's been here every single day since you recovered. He's probably next door in the spare parlour right now.'

'Why didn't anyone tell me?' I asked, rising from the armchair where I had been made to sit with a blanket over my knees.

Aunt Hilda and Rachel, who was sitting by the fire knitting, glanced at each other.

'It was for your own good,' Rachel said. 'You're still very frail. For goodness' sake, you've just recovered from a six-month coma – you shouldn't be worried by things.'

'I should have been told,' I said, walking to the door. I turned at it. 'This is important. We need to hear what the man has to say.'

As my aunt had guessed, Cyril Baker was waiting in the spare parlour, sitting on a sofa that was covered with a dust cloth. He was reading a leather-bound book, which had the word 'Good' in the title. I had to look twice at him, so remarkable was the transformation from the pale, superior man I had encountered before. At first glance one would think he was a Mexican, or an Italian, so dark was his hair. Until you noticed the deathly pallor of his skin.

'You've changed,' I blurted, holding out my hand to him. He took it; his own was cold, clammy. Out of the corner of my eye I could see that Aunt Hilda and Rachel had followed me.

'None of your friends think so.'

'I mean in appearance.'

31

'Appearances are the least of it. I'm a different man. My heart has opened.'

I took away my hand, finding it hard to bear his touch any longer. 'You'll excuse my friends if they are a little mistrustful,' I said. 'Are we expected to just take your word for this transformation? Forgive me, but kidnap and murder are the least of your crimes.'

He smiled, his pale eyes shining. 'I was bad. I know it. Bad to my very heart. But – Kit, I saved you. I visited one of the doctors your friends took you to. He said you were as good as dead – past saving. I refused to believe him. I vowed never to give up. So I found Walter Silas. I gave him the money for his invention. He has been working on it for three months.'

I could have sworn Baker was sincere. Or else he was a very good actor. How could I *really* tell?

'Thank you.' I paused. 'But why go to such trouble for me? The last few times we've met you tried to kill me.'

Mr Baker rose to his feet and brushed a speck of dust off his perfectly pressed linen trousers. 'I told you. I have changed. But I don't expect you to just take my word for it. I want to *show* you.'

⁖⊱⊰⁖

Sometime later we stood in the central docks, near a huge corrugated-iron warehouse that was silhouetted against the sun. It was one of the many shops and stores that lined the wharf. Despite the protests of my friends, we had come here, to San Francisco's main shipping port.

'Do not judge me too harshly for what you are about to see,' Baker said, as we stood outside the warehouse. 'It is horrible . . .'

He pushed the door open and we entered. As soon as I stepped in, I wanted to gag as the awful smell knocked me back. It was a mix of urine, decaying meat, sweat – the misery of too many human beings packed into too small a space. It was dark inside and it took a few seconds for my eyes to see anything. Pulleys and lifting equipment hung from the ceiling. Looking down, I saw a swarm of human beings. It was like opening the front of a beehive and peering in. People sat, crawled, crouched, lay semi-naked on the floor. Most of them were Chinese. Some of them were chained about the ankles; others had their hands roped together. They were mostly men, looking at the strangers at the door with blank, resigned faces, although I did see some women and one baby.

One man glanced at me and then flinched away, as if I might hit him. He was squatting next to a boy scarcely more than ten years old. I guessed he was the child's father. The boy had cropped hair and bright eyes, the only eyes that looked at me with some spark. For an instant he reminded me of Yin, my friend whom I had left behind in China. She too, I remembered, had been captured and transported across the seas like this, before we had rescued her.

I remembered that I had seen the hold where these poor Chinese coolies were transported over the seas to America. I had seen the spots of blood and the hooks and chains where they were tethered to the walls. I had suspected the Bakers were involved in this evil trade. Now I had the evidence.

'Don't be too harsh on me,' Cyril said, as we stood there silent and disgusted, taking in all the squalor.

'Harsh?' Rachel asked through clenched teeth. 'How could we be too harsh? You're truly revolting. Below contempt.'

'I agree with you,' Cyril said.

'You do?'

'With all my heart. This trade in coolies is evil.'

'Slavery,' Rachel hissed.

'Not slavery, bonded labour,' Cyril replied. 'I make no apologies for it. But you must understand the difference. It is *legal*. Bonded labourers like these have built America. Some of my coolies built the great western railways. These men will be free when they have repaid their debts to us.'

'Will that ever happen?' I asked.

'It is hard – their debts are high; the cost of their passage from China is huge.'

I shuddered, recalling that ghastly hold where men like these had been chained.

'I expect they're the kind of debts that can never be paid off,' Rachel said.

'You're so right. The way of business.' Baker tried to smile at Rachel, but she turned her face away and crouched down before a small boy chained to an older man.

'This is how it was,' Baker continued, 'with me and my brother Cecil. We made a fortune from human flesh, among other things. But a new wind is blowing. Once my brother and I had ten warehouses like this –' He broke off, choking a little on the foul vapour in the shed, a handkerchief over his nose. 'Please come outside. I do not feel so well in here . . . Please just give me a moment.'

Wiping off a spot of sweat above his lips, Baker walked across to the overseer, a Chinaman with a curling rawhide whip. I saw their conversation in a kind of dumb show. I could see their movements, but not hear their voices. He was saying something to the man. The overseer seemed to be arguing. Baker raised his voice and for a moment I thought the overseer was about to hit him. Then he stepped back and, hanging his head, the overseer nodded. Whatever it was about, Mr Baker had won his point.

The air didn't feel so fresh when we were out on the dock with the tang of salt tainted with blood. We stood outside the warehouse, not knowing what to say. I looked at Mr Baker and couldn't understand how someone could be a human and inflict such misery on other humans.

'How could you? Children. Fathers. People. Just like you and me,' Rachel murmured finally.

'Yes.' Mr Baker turned to her. 'It has taken death to make me understand that.'

'What do you mean?'

'These men, these Chinamen or Indians or negroes. When I started in business, I never saw them as humans. They were units. Of profit. Of gold. And later of beautiful things that I could collect and own and treasure. You see, I thought I was special. Only *I* would appreciate these lovely things. You must understand – I bought the finest art from all over the world. Such beauty in the hands of Cyril Baker, the son of an ordinary servant –' He came to a sudden stop.

'You're heartless, Mr Baker,' Rachel said. Her eyes were glowing with indignation, her face set. 'You see these men as coolies, as not quite human. Well, I see *you* as a subhuman.'

She turned her back on him and marched into the path of an oncoming dray, which had to swerve, the driver cursing her. 'Come, Isaac. We want nothing to do with this man.'

Isaac followed, the others in his footsteps. I found it hard to move. My mind was clouded. Some things were clearer, much clearer, but I couldn't *act*. The others marched off.

'Kit.' Waldo turned round to me. 'Come on.'

I hesitated.

'Listen. I beg you, listen.' Cyril held his white-gloved hands up in the air. 'Please, I've changed.'

'I am listening,' I said.

'What are you talking about, Kit?' Waldo strode back to me and tugged me by the arm. 'Since when do you listen to anyone?'

'Please, Waldo. I want to hear Mr Baker out.'

My friends and father had stopped and were turning towards us. I saw alarm on Father's face and remembered he hadn't wanted to come here. He had wanted me back home, resting in bed.

'Miss Salter, Professor Salter, please listen to me. I am a changed man. Do you see those carts over there?' He pointed to the line of drays moving towards us.

'Get on with it, man,' Aunt Hilda said impatiently.

'They are coming to take these Chinamen. These bonded labourers. I am setting them free. I have given them each fifty dollars.'

Waldo whistled sarcastically. 'Fifty dollars.'

'Yes, you are right. I will make it a hundred. They will be going to a hostel right here in San Francisco, Chinatown.'

He seemed to be speaking at least some portion of the truth, for as he spoke the Chinese were herded out of the shed by the whip-toting overseer. A straggling line of them moved towards the horses and carts. They'd had their chains removed. Mr Baker called to the overseer and each man was given a leather pouch. I saw one open his, and saw the glint of silver inside. Most of them were silent. But the small boy was whooping and hanging on to his father's hand.

We watched silently as the coolies clambered aboard the carts. They seemed bewildered, mostly mute and resigned to this new twist in their fate. One boy, who'd had his leg irons removed, had a wild look in his eye. He was sixteen or seventeen, fit, less emaciated than most of the others. He clutched the pouch as if he would never be parted from it, and hung over the edge of the cart. I guessed he would take the first opportunity to run, and would melt into the city of San Francisco. Never to be seen again.

'Is this a trick, Mr Baker?' Waldo asked. 'How do you expect us to believe you will free these men? You could be just sending them to another prison.'

'Trust me.'

'You? Why should we? You're the most slippery creature I've ever met. Aside from your brother, that is.'

'True.' Cyril was sweating again; the handkerchief moved to dab at his lip. 'Give me one chance. Just one chance. I've changed and I want to tell you my story.'

'I think we should give him a chance,' I murmured. 'He has set these people free.'

My father spoke, his voice uncertain. 'I agree with my daughter. After all, this man saved Kit's life.'

The drays and carts were driving off now in a flurry of dust. Dozens of those skinny arms hung over the sides of the carts. I turned away; there were so many unfair things in the world. I was so helpless. This man beside me, this Mr Baker, had done so much to make the world a worse place. I don't know if I will be able to do much, when I am older and able to take my place in society, but I do hope that *I* don't increase the sum of human misery.

Abruptly Cyril Baker's mood changed. He wasn't listening any more. His eyes darted around.

'Where is Mr Chen?' he asked.

'Who?'

'My overseer. The man with the whip.'

'He has gone,' Aunt Hilda said. 'I saw him leave in that.' She pointed to a cart that was going in the opposite direction to the line of dray horses. It was moving off at a fine clip. As we watched, it curved round a bend in the road and disappeared.

'Disaster!' Cyril exploded. 'Quick. We have no time to lose.'

'Why?' Aunt Hilda asked. 'What's wrong?'

'No time. Hurry.' As we watched, Cyril called for his carriage and bundled in, urging us in after him. Waldo protested, but I got in and the others followed me. Baker had something auburn-haired in his hands, which he put on his head. It was a wig, a silky, long-haired wig.

As the driver cracked his whip and the horses raced off, Cyril Baker transformed before our eyes. He peeled off the black moustache. Gone was the pale-skinned Spaniard. In his place was a ginger man, an Irishman perhaps.

Cyril leaned out of the carriage and shouted at his driver. 'Faster!' he yelled. 'Not the normal way. I want Ho Chen Alley.'

❧ Chapter Six ❧

The carriage hurtled out of the port, up the hill and twisted sharply to the right. Shops and warehouses thundered by and then we were out of the shipping district and charging through the traffic. Drays and other coaches swept out of our way and soon we veered off the main roads, going deeper and deeper into the dark alleys behind the splendid facade of San Francisco.

A firecracker exploded above us as we pelted past a shop gilded with black and red dragons. We were in San Francisco's Chinatown. For an instant I was transported thousands of miles across the sea, back to China, by the names of the shops: Chow Yun Hed, Yeng Lee, Wang Ho. Scarlet lanterns painted with delicate oriental brush-strokes swung high in the air.

'I feel strange,' I whispered to Waldo as the carriage threw me against him. 'Like we're back in Shanghai or—'

'Frisco's Chinatown. Biggest in the world. Pretty impressive, huh?' he replied, not meeting my eye.

Cyril had spent much of the ride looking through the

window at the back of the carriage, checking for pursuit. It was an unusual design to have a window so placed. Now he hung out of the door of the carriage and shouted something to the coachman, who lurched to a stop.

'It's better we walk the rest of the way,' Mr Baker said, his hand straying to his gingery wig. 'It'll make it harder for him.'

'Make it harder for whom?' Aunt Hilda demanded. 'What is all this cloak-and-dagger stuff for?'

Baker didn't reply. Instead he turned into a door that said COME IN AND STRIKE LUCKY GOLD. We passed through a Fan Tan gambling saloon crowded with Chinamen smoking and dealing cards. There were one or two women, in tight, high-necked Chinese dresses, serving drinks. Before I had the time to see more, Baker had gone through the gambling den and ducked out of a side entrance. We followed him down an alley till we came to an even smaller alley. Baker stopped in front of a small door with no sign but plenty of peeling blue paint. He selected a key from a bunch and opened the lock. Stepping aside, he invited us in.

'Hardly discreet,' he muttered to himself, 'charging through Chinatown with a pack of foreigners. Still, can't be helped.'

We tramped up a dingy, unlit staircase which smelt of damp. A tenement – the kind of boarding house where you would find several, indeed, dozens of families huddled together. Cyril stopped at a landing and opened another door.

What a shock! I had expected a dingy room, a parlour maybe, for a cheap Chinese lodging house. But it was nothing of the sort. We had entered a world of taste and comfort. Deep leather armchairs, a glossy mahogany table, telegraph equipment, glass-fronted bookcases lined with leather-bound tomes. A shelf of pea-green vases shimmered near the window.

Careful not to upset the vase nearby, I took a seat next to Mr Baker, who had slumped in an armchair and covered his head with his hands.

'Who are you running from, Cyril?' I asked.

'Isn't that obvious?'

'Not to me,' Aunt Hilda muttered.

'It's Cecil. My brother.'

Our silence hung in the air, thick with distrust.

'Cecil? Your twin?' Aunt Hilda said finally. 'I thought you were inseparable.'

Cyril raised his hand to his head and took off the ginger wig. With a sigh, he tossed it onto the table.

'It used to be that way,' he replied. 'We were Tweedledum and Tweedledee. I was Cecil's shadow. We thought as one, acted as one, got rich – fantastically rich – as one. But all that has changed.'

'How so?'

Cyril hung his head. I could see the pinkish line of his scalp where the black dye had not penetrated.

'He has gone too far – even for me.'

'What has he done? It must have been truly awful to offend *your* morals,' Aunt Hilda said. 'Has he tried to kill Queen Victoria?'

Cecil did not reply.

'So now we're meant to believe he is after you?' she went on.

'He is trying to kill me,' Cyril said. Nervous, he bent down and picked up his wig. 'My brother does nothing by halves. When the overseer disappeared from the warehouse, I feared he had gone to my brother. As you can imagine, he doesn't want me to set our coolies free – that is why –' His hand flew to his wig again. 'All this, the moustache, the wig. I'm having a set of false teeth made.'

It was an odd coincidence, but the six of us – me, my friends and my aunt and father – were sitting ranged against Cyril Baker. For a moment it struck me that it was like a trial. He was the defendant, in the dock, and we the jury who might hold the gift of life. We might convict, or pardon.

I stood up and went over to Cyril and knelt before his chair, while the others looked at me in shock. I could understand their bewilderment. This man was a criminal, an outlaw from human feeling, and here I was kneeling

44

before him. I believed I was doing the right thing. An inner voice told me to give him a chance.

'This is much too confusing,' I said. 'You're giving us snippets of your story. Tell us everything. Tell us where it all began.'

'Very well – this is my confession. The confession of a very sick man. Yes . . .' for Baker had seen the look on Waldo's face, 'I am dying. You probably think good riddance. But if I am dying before my time, so too is your friend Kit. We are both dying of the same disease.'

Waldo's face flushed furiously. 'Quiet!' he said. 'Kit is better. We won't listen to your filthy lies.'

I wanted to tell Waldo to calm down, for I knew Baker was telling the truth. I *was* sick, dying. We had caught the same disease in the Himalayas. All three of us. Me, Kit Salter, and the twins Cecil and Cyril Baker. The brothers had drunk greedily from the sacred fountain in the mountain paradise of Shambala and it had turned to poison in their bodies. The water was a blessing for those who were ready for it, conferring immortality and eternal youth. For those who were not ready, it was a curse. Though I hadn't drunk from the fountain, I too had become infected by the waters. I had breathed in tiny particles of moisture; I had ingested droplets of dew through my skin. Inside me there was a worm of disease. I was not as sick as the Bakers. But, make no mistake, I too was slowly decaying from the inside.

The rot buried inside me had come to the surface in the temple in China when I had encountered the holy bones of the long-dead sage. The sacred Chinese bones and the Himalayan disease had fought for supremacy, each one claiming mastery of me, Kit Salter. They had clashed mightily inside my frail human body. I was not strong enough for this battle; the result of so much power churning inside me was that I had fallen into a deep coma – I slept unaware, for many months.

Thankfully, the electricity had woken me from the coma. But the Himalayan bug still festered in me. I was living under a suspended sentence of death. I knew the truth of this. But, despite the fact they had seen me in a coma, my friends refused to accept it.

'I ought to take you by the collar and throw you into the street,' Waldo said, jumping up and moving menacingly towards Cyril.

'Bravo, Waldo,' Aunt Hilda said. 'We aren't afraid of you, Baker, or your thugs.'

Cyril Baker cast a curious look at me, as if waiting for me to speak on his behalf. But I kept quiet.

'Very well, I will not talk about your niece again,' he said to Aunt Hilda. 'All I will say is that I see death plain and clear. It stalks me as I sleep. As I sit here. I know I will not live much longer. Weeks. Perhaps days. This knowledge has cleared my head.

'I am a condemned man. I am going to hell where I—'

'I'm not a vengeful person,' Rachel interrupted, 'but for what you have done, hell seems pretty fair.'

He looked her straight in the eye for a moment. 'I don't deny it. But – I am trying. I want to say sorry.'

'Sorry!' Aunt Hilda said. 'Easiest word in the language.'

Baker rose from his armchair and stood before us. He was very thin, I could see. Such was his pallor that he looked closer to death than life. He had been ghastly-looking the very first time I had glimpsed him in London. But now he was for the grave, a walking ghost, despite his dyed black hair.

'I come as you know from ordinary working stock. My father was a labourer, a simple country boy. He obtained a job in a great house as a footman. My brother, Cecil, and I sometimes used to sneak into the house. We weren't let beyond the kitchen, but once, just once, we gave our father the slip and roamed about.

'The Persian carpets, the crystal chandeliers, the shining mahogany tables, the oil paintings gleaming from the walls . . . Envy bloomed inside us, as well as determination. We made a vow. We would be rich.

'We were clever boys, and moreover we dared to dream of a life beyond "our station". I don't think we were bad when we began. But we were ruthless. And soon, yes, evil set into our hearts. I won't bore you with how we made

47

our fortune. There were crimes. We invested our profits in a little scheme to ship slaves from the Congo in Africa to the West Indies. That was very profitable, and soon we branched out – human flesh, opium, vice of all kinds. We were open-minded about our business opportunities. By the time we were forty Cecil and I were rich – fabulously, stinking rich.

'But that was not enough for Cecil. He had to have more. We became great collectors. Financed expeditions around the whole empire searching for treasure. Ming vases, jade Buddhas, Tintoretto paintings. We might have been the greatest collectors in the history of the world. We weren't bound by a single continent or style, you see. We became experts, seeking out the lovely and the rare from across the globe.'

'This is making my stomach turn,' Aunt Hilda said. 'What has all this to do with my niece Kit?'

Baker held up a trembling hand. 'It's obvious, isn't it? My brother is pursuing her. He wants her dead – no . . . worse.'

Aunt Hilda ignored this threat to me. 'Your boasting—'

'I am not boasting, just explaining. If you don't understand my brother – well, how can you hope to resist him? I said we were the greatest collectors the world had ever seen. That's gone, at least for me. I've given it all away!'

'What?'

'It's gone. All gone. My half, at least. Pearls, paintings, gold, bonds.'

'All your money?' Aunt Hilda asked.

'Pretty much.'

'Where? Where's it gone?'

'Hospitals, orphanages, ragged schools. I'm a regular do-gooder now. I've set up a fund right here in Chinatown. I am trying to say sorry. I know I can never make it right, not with the wrong I've done. But, hell, I'm *trying*.'

'You expect us to *believe* you?' Waldo asked.

'I can take you to the orphanage right here in Chinatown—'

'Your brother,' Rachel interrupted. 'You said he hates the idea of giving your money away.'

Baker sighed. 'Cecil has always been the leader. From the time we were boys, he led and I followed. He's a stubborn soul. And now, well . . . he knows we're damned. The elixir of life didn't save us, nor the Book of Bones. Nothing has saved us. But he won't give it all away. He won't say sorry. He won't *beg for forgiveness*. Cecil Baker would ride up to the gates of hell and try to make a deal with the devil.'

There was silence after this as we all thought of Cecil Baker and his twin, Cyril, the supposedly reformed man who sat in front of us. Had he really shaken off evil? Could a soul so steeped in wickedness really change? But it was something Cyril had said earlier that was bothering me.

'Why does your brother want me?' I asked him.

Rachel let out a gasp. Cyril looked at me for a moment then his eyes moved uneasily away. He couldn't look at me. Couldn't answer my question straight.

'I know what you're thinking,' he said into the silence. 'You're thinking this is some kind of trick. Believe me, my brother hasn't spoken to me since the day I announced I was giving all my money away. We've been inseparable since we were in breeches. Now he will not see me, or read my letters. He considers me a traitor.

'This morning someone tried to knife me. If Rumbelow hadn't fought him off, I would be dead.'

'I'm mighty sorry for your family problems, but I don't see how it is any of our concern,' Waldo said.

'Don't you see? My problems matter more than anything to you. Specially to Kit,' Cyril replied.

I didn't say a word as my name came out of his mouth like a bullet. Again he was claiming that I was in danger, but again he was being purposely vague about *exactly* what the danger was.

Waldo flinched. 'I thought we'd agreed to keep Kit out of it.'

'This concerns Kit. It is life and death to her. You see, I know what my brother is planning.'

'I don't buy this threat-to-Kit business . . . You have always been fascinated with Kit. Don't know why,' Waldo said, with a quick glance at me. 'This feels like one more ruse.' He got up and took a step towards the door. 'Sir, it is time for us to leave.'

'Stop!' Cyril yelled. 'You must believe me. You must come with me to Arizona.'

'Arizona?'

'The Grand Canyon. It is where my brother plans the ceremony. I don't know exactly what, but—'

'You've lost your mind,' Waldo said, moving closer to the door. 'We're going.'

'Kit, look at your left arm.' Cyril stood up to bar his way. 'The soft spot above your elbow.'

I looked down and gasped. A mark had appeared on my arm. A pattern of blotches, like birth marks or beauty spots bleeding together. But this was no pretty thing. It was a snake. A black snake speckled with brown blotches was curling towards my forearm.

As I looked at the cursed thing in horror, Mr Baker lifted his arm. White gloves covered his hands up to his wrists. He rolled up his left shirtsleeve to the elbow and we all saw the vile thing.

A black snake, the mirror image of the one on my own arm.

❧ Chapter Seven ❧

I looked from my snake brand to Cecil's markings and my head exploded with pain. Flaring lights burst before my eyes. I screamed. Everyone turned to look at me. Through a white glare I saw my father stuttering and Aunt Hilda goggling at me, her jaw hanging open.

'Pull yourself together, Kit,' she snapped finally.

I could hardly speak, the pain in my head was so intense. My tongue felt bloated and stuck to the back of my throat.

'Not feeling well. Going back . . . hotel. Lie down,' I managed.

'I'll go with you,' Rachel said.

'No.'

'I'll go,' Waldo said. 'She needs a man with her.'

'I will accompany Kit home, no arguments,' my father said. 'In fact, I think we should all leave right away.'

'Please, don't be alarmed. I felt it too when I saw the mark for the first time. Please, I can explain.' Cyril Baker bobbed up in front of the door, trying to hold us back. 'I

52

need to tell you about my brother's plans. I need to tell you about the tablet.'

My father's face was unusually stern. He was desperate to be out of this luxurious little prison, desperate to have me back in safety. But Mr Baker was equally desperate. Maniacally, he babbled on about conspiracy and treasure, while my father and friends tried to leave.

I sat back and listened, though my mind was clouded by terror and I could not take my eyes from the snake on my arm. Why had I not seen it before? Had it just appeared? Was this ugly brand a symbol of my damnation?

That was the most terrifying thing. I could not get the thought out of my mind that Mr Baker and I bore the brand of the snake for the same reason. We both carried a cursed bug inside us. Was this now slithering out of our insides? Had it appeared on our skin to show our leprous condition to the world?

It had to be. The snakes on our arms had to be linked to the canker in our souls, the disease eating at our guts. Why else would Cyril and I share the same brand? If that was the case, I was truly damned. The snake was the poison I had been infected with in the mountains of India, now made a horrible fleshy reality. I had strayed where I shouldn't – been trapped by my curiosity time and again. True, I had become entangled in the Bakers' foul web, but my own hot-headed pride had played its part in my doom.

The snake was the sign of all this, branded on my own soft flesh.

⸺ৡৣ⸺

Back at the boarding house I slept for several hours and awoke feeling wearier than before. A glance at my arm told me that the snake had slept too – it hadn't vanished as I'd hoped. I had a large window with a comfortable ledge on which to perch. Down below, a curious mixture of people paraded the streets of San Francisco. There were the fine ladies, wearing the latest fashions from New York and Paris, some with ridiculously large bustles, as if they had grown two bottoms. Then there were the toughs in red checked shirts, blue trousers tucked into their boots. Miners and cowboys mingled with the best of San Francisco high society. This was a true frontier town, the sort where anything goes.

As I watched I tried to ignore the tension in my mind, which was building up to a screaming headache.

Drearily I went over the conversation with Cyril. He had talked more after he'd shown us the brand of the snake on his arm. Everyone, my aunt and Waldo included, had grown quiet at the sight. Cyril had told us he believed that all the objects the Bakers had sought were linked in 'lines of power'.

There were five such objects the Bakers knew about,

though they believed more were scattered around the world. The first one they had acquired and kept in their castle, an ancient Celtic amulet. But then I'd turned up on their trail and things had begun to go wrong. They'd been thwarted in their desire to seize the oldest book in the world, the Egyptian writing of Ptah Hotep. They had not managed to bring back a bottle of the elixir of life from the Himalayas. Finally, the bones of Bodhidharma from the caves above the Shaolin temple in China had eluded them.

The Bakers believed that they had identified one last object. The most holy, ancient and powerful of them all. It was a marble tablet, inscribed with ancient hieroglyphs, eerie stick figures and writing, the meaning of which was lost in the mists of time. Some believed that this tablet was Anasazi, belonging to the 'ancient ones', a lost tribe who had lived in the desert of Arizona many thousands of years ago. The Hopi Indians, who were rumoured to have the tablet, believed it had been given to them by their god when the tribe emerged from the womb of the world in the Grand Canyon.

The Bakers had learned about the existence of this tablet from their network of informers. Cecil Baker had become obsessed. He wanted to know everything about it, so for years he had studied shamanism, the magical priestly rites of the Indians. For an outsider, he had becoming very powerful. So powerful that these days Cecil could walk barefoot over hot coals or lie naked on an iceberg. He was all but a shaman himself.

Yet, despite all his mystical power, Cecil Baker was cursed. His magic was useless against the disease eating him from the inside, the brand of the snake on his arm. (Yes, like his brother and I, he was branded.) But he saw one way out. The Anasazi tablet. He believed that if he had the tablet he would be able to cheat the gates of hell. He would become immeasurably powerful. I asked many questions, but I wasn't told *exactly* how this tablet would help Cecil trick his fate. But in some way, his brother was sure, Cecil believed this tablet would be his salvation.

Cecil sought this relic in the Grand Canyon, a huge area of towering cliffs and gorges in the Arizona desert.

His face contorting with desperation, Cyril Baker had told us he believed his brother had gone mad. He'd become obsessed, consumed by a lust for the tablet. He had hatched plans too dreadful even for his adoring twin to go along with. Cecil would use the tablet to make himself invincible – and into the bargain he would kill me.

'Please, please believe me. We must stop my brother. We must find the tablet first or Cecil will be unstoppable,' Cyril had begged.

'How?' we had asked. How could we find this legendary and fiercely guarded tablet in the Grand Canyon, a wilderness of cliffs? All Cyril had replied was that he had the same clues as his brother to its whereabouts. With our help, *he* could get there first.

Now sitting at my bedroom window, with my head throbbing, I thought over Cyril's story. On the face of it, there was no reason to trust him. He had always hated me. He had kidnapped me, shot at me, tricked me. I was supposed to believe in his sudden volte-face. Now he was acting as if all he wanted to do was save my life.

Why were the Baker brothers so interested in me anyway? Right from the start of our involvement I had the impression they were focusing on *me*. This feeling was stronger than ever. Cyril had even hinted as much, saying his brother was fascinated by me. That he wanted me, Kit Salter, dead.

Why me? I kept turning the question over in my mind. It had become a niggle, an itch that I had to scratch.

Did we really have a chance to find the Anasazi tablet, with a madman after it?

⌘

After I had turned our dilemma uselessly over in my head for some time, I went downstairs to the parlour. My friends, father and aunt were all there, arguing.

Father wanted to stay here and rest. Waldo backed him up fiercely. He could not lead us into any more danger, he said. But the rest, including the cautious Rachel, surprisingly, argued that we had to find this *thing* lurking in the Grand Canyon. Rachel told me, in a private moment, that she felt some terrible curse hanging over my head. Above all she wanted to 'set me free'.

In the end the argument was unresolved. Waldo, Isaac and Aunt Hilda were to set off once again, back to a slum area of the city. Mr Baker had told them he would prove he'd become a different man. He was going to show them a couple of the charitable projects on which he had spent his dirty money. I wanted to go with them, but was ordered back to my room. For once I didn't protest too much. Rachel was staying behind too. She was to be my jailor.

So I went back to my room and lay down, while Rachel knitted in the corner. After a while, I slept. My dreams were full of twisting snakes: glistening black cobras, adders bright as blades of spring grass, pythons flickering towards me with their eyes glinting. Snakes, snakes and more snakes. I was stepping on a pile of them. A small grass snake detached itself from the heap and began crawling up my leg. 'No!' I shouted in horror, backing away. But the thing was on me, wriggling wetly up my leg.

I couldn't shake it off.

When I woke up, my hair was damp with sweat and the front of my blouse wet. Waldo was standing over me, his blond hair golden in the twilight.

'Mr Baker thinks we should move,' he said. 'He thinks

even another night here would be dangerous. He thinks his brother may know where we are.'

I groaned. Waldo took a seat at the other end of the bedroom, as far away from me as possible. Rachel had vanished. Was it my imagination or had Waldo become distant since I'd recovered? He hardly ever looked me in the eye now. The ease in each other's company, the fun we had teasing each other – that had gone.

'Waldo,' I said, 'have I done something to offend you?'

'Whatever gave you that idea?'

'I don't know. I think you've been . . . kind of . . . avoiding me.'

Waldo flushed and looked down at his boots.

'You get the funniest ideas,' he said, still not meeting my eye. He clearly didn't want to talk about whatever it was that was bothering him. 'Look, I want to talk about something real. This whole Baker thing – this Grand Canyon idea – it's dangerous. Your father has asked me to have a serious talk with you.'

My heart stopped for an instant, and I found *I* didn't want to look at Waldo.

'About what?'

'Our future . . .' He blushed. For some stupid reason, I was blushing too. 'I mean *your* future.'

'Oh.'

'He wants to see if I can talk you out of this scheme.

This mad scheme to go west – and the Grand Canyon. It's madness. Chasms. Gorges. Wild raging rivers. Hardly explored. I mean, what can you be thinking of?'

The old fight had gone out of me. Once I had been so sure. But now . . . everything was hazy . . . the snake and Baker's evil presence looming over us . . . If he had found out where we lived, even now we could be in danger. It was as if I was walking through a land where everything was coated in a layer of mist. Except Waldo, who was shining bright before me, his eyes sky blue.

'How was your visit?' I asked, changing the subject. 'Has Mr Baker told us the truth?'

'Ye-es,' Waldo admitted, looking down at the floor.

'And?'

'There was a school, very well furnished, and the children were learning. They hail Cyril Baker as their saviour.'

'And those poor Chinese labourers?'

'He has set them free. With a few dollars in their pockets.'

'So he really has had a change of heart.'

'Or maybe he's just decided to invest a few thousand dollars into tricking us. That's not a lot of money for a man of Baker's wealth.'

'You're such a cynic, Waldo. I believe him. I think he has repented.'

He glanced at me as I said that, a burning look that made me feel suddenly miserable.

'You're always so restless, Kit. Always so keen to put your life in danger – and the lives of others.'

'No,' I said softly. 'I think Cyril Baker has changed, deep in his soul. I think he knows he has done many evil things and is doomed and . . .'

'Yes, yes.' Waldo rose from his chair. 'I can see I'm not going to change your mind. I suppose we will be setting off for Arizona – and more madness.' He moved towards the door, turning his back to me. 'I will have to tell your father I cannot reason with you.'

'Waldo!'

From the door he grunted, without turning round.

'Please. Waldo. Please, come here.'

'What is it now?'

'I want to show you something.'

He came slowly, as if pulled against his wishes, to the spot where I was curled up on the window ledge. I was wearing a maroon velvet skirt with a blouse, which had long lace sleeves that came to my wrists. Not my choice of clothes – Rachel had purchased them sometime when I was ill. Now, calmly as I could, I rolled up my sleeve.

Waldo was standing very near, so close I could feel his hot breath.

'What am I supposed to be looking at?' His words were impatient, but he was very pale and standing very still.

Wordlessly, I tugged at the sleeve and turned my arm over to show him the soft flesh under my elbow.

He grabbed at my wrist and held it so tight it hurt. I bit back the pain. Then he dropped it and moved away, as if scalded. He was trembling.

The brand of the snake had moved. It had crept up my arm while I slept and now lay curled under my elbow. Even as I talked to Waldo, it seemed as if the tiny tongue flickered.

'It's looking for my heart,' I said. 'The snake's trying to kill me.'

❧ Chapter Eight ❧

We moved to another boarding house that night. It was Isaac who spotted the cowboy with the curling black moustache lounging against the gas lamp opposite us. He wore brown leather boots and a studded belt. The skin on his face was gnarled and wrinkled. Something about his thick, repulsive lips reminded me of someone.

We wouldn't have thought anything of it, but when I looked out two hours later he was still there. Standing in exactly the same spot. It was sinister. It made Cyril Baker's warning that his brother was looking for us more real. Waldo and Father both insisted we move. So we paid Mr Hilton and sneaked out of a back door. Mr Hilton had organised a carriage for us, which would take us to lodgings run by a friend of his.

I felt like a criminal, flitting in darkness from our hotel. We changed horses twice before we got to our new hotel on the edge of the city. That night I slept uneasily. The only good thing about our move was that we had already packed. It would make our departure for Arizona in the morning much quicker.

Yes, in the end even Father had agreed I had to go. The sight of the sinister full-lipped man stalking us had tipped him over the edge. He no longer thought I was safe in San Francisco.

Aunt Hilda had purchased some travelling clothes for us. Light, tough cotton skirts, calico blouses and large hats to shade the glare of the desert sun. It promised to be a gruelling journey, travelling by rail and stagecoach to the Grand Canyon. We would have to cross deserts and mountains, going through territory that only the toughest pioneers had braved before us. But first we would traverse the gentle California hills.

⁂

Before we left, something rather sad happened. We were all ready to depart at first light, hasty breakfast eaten, the carriage pulled up outside the hotel, when we noticed Father had disappeared.

'Go up to his room and stir the old fool,' my aunt said to Waldo. 'We have to be off before Cecil Baker gets wind of our whereabouts.'

'I'll go,' I said, glaring at Aunt Hilda, for I found her habit of calling her brother and *my* father 'fool' offensive.

I trekked to his room and knocked on the door, but

there was no answer. I knocked again. I tried the handle, which turned easily. But there was something blocking the door and, pushing hard, I was unable to move it. I heaved with all my might and finally the door opened. I went in to find Father lying spread-eagled on the floor.

'Father!'

For an awful moment I thought he'd had a heart attack. But he was breathing, short, shallow puffs. I moved his hat, which had fallen off, and I sat down by him. Gently, I lifted his hand. It was clammy, unpleasant to touch.

'Father,' I repeated.

He opened his eyes. They were flickering wildly over the room as if seeking some invisible enemy. They flitted over me, as if he didn't recognise me, then came back and focused. I saw the relief on his face.

'Kit?'

'What is it, Father? What happened?'

'I must have fainted.'

Breathing heavily, my father stood up. His legs were weak and wobbled. He only made it as far as the chair, which stood in front of the oak writing table, before he collapsed.

'Are you quite all right?'

'I'm fine, my dear.'

'Father, are you nervous about the journey?'

'No. Not at all. I know . . .' He paused. 'I know we are

in the best hands with your aunt. Such a brave woman. An explorer, a . . .'

He paused again, his thoughts drifting away. Looking at him, I knew he was lying. He was scared. He didn't want to come with us, but would make himself. Duty was very important to Father. Hadn't he just said he would never leave me to fend for myself again? At the sight of him crumpled up on the chair like a very old man, my heart flipped over. I didn't want to play a trick on him, but for his own sake I had to.

'Father, prepare yourself. I have some very bad news.'

I removed a piece of paper from my coat pocket. 'This is an urgent telegram. It has just arrived.'

'What? What?'

'It's from the museum.'

'What museum?'

'Your museum, Father, the Pitt in Oxford. They say the Ancient Egypt section is in turmoil. And they don't know what to do with the Early Hebrew exhibition. They are in a mess, Father. They beg you to come back. Only you can sort it out, they say.'

'Oh dear, oh dear.' He paused. 'NO. I cannot do it.'

'They're begging you, Papa.'

'My place is with you, Kit.'

'Father, they say the museum is on the point of collapse. You must save it!'

He was torn. I could see it. His hands tugged at his hair and he chewed his lips.

'It's collapsing?'

'Yes, collapsing.'

'But you're my . . . my Kit . . . How can I leave you?'

'You mustn't feel guilty. I will have Aunt Hilda and Waldo. I will be quite safe.'

I could see the relief in his eyes. After another ten minutes of persuasion I managed to gain his consent to return to Oxford and the stricken museum. Luckily he hadn't asked to see the telegram. If he had, he would have found it was a list of the items Aunt Hilda had bought for our trip.

As we embraced and said our tearful goodbyes, Father pressed something into my hand. I opened my palm when I was outside in the corridor and saw something golden glimmering in it. It was a heart-shaped locket on a gold chain. I opened it and inside was a miniature of a young woman. She had a lovely oval face and wild auburn hair. But it wasn't her beauty that arrested me. It was the fire in her eyes. Usually the faces of ladies in miniatures are placid and a bit dull. But the painter hadn't been able to hide this woman's spirit.

It was my mother. Tabitha. The locket was a beautiful thing, one that I had never seen before. I hurried down to the waiting carriage, my eyes awash with tears.

I had a job persuading Aunt Hilda that the museum was in trouble and Father couldn't come with us. But finally she accepted it:

'He's such a lily-liver that he was probably glad of the excuse to go home.'

There was a bit of truth in her words, but that didn't make me less furious with her for speaking of her brother like that. Father has always had a difficult relationship with his bully of a sister. He is so bruised by years of schoolroom battering that it takes a lot of provocation to make him stand up to her. Leave him alone, I wanted to say to Aunt Hilda. I know she is fond of him, but she is such a stubborn bull-like person that she has no understanding of tact. The journey would be easier without the burden of protecting my father from my aunt.

I made the carriage stop at the telegraph station so I could send a message to my father's colleagues in Oxford. Tactfully I told them that Papa was returning for his health, but that I would appreciate it if they pretended they could not manage without him. My father is so dreamy he would probably have forgotten why he was returning by the time his ship docked in Liverpool.

Cyril Baker was waiting for us at the ferry station, hiding, it seemed, behind some bales of cotton. He was as ghostlike as ever. He seemed to float onto the boat, in his cream linen suit, similar to the one he wore in Egypt when I first set eyes upon him. He had taken off the ginger wig, and the black dye in his hair seemed to be fading. I noticed there was a rash on his neck, burning red spots creeping up to his chin.

'This is a grand old boat,' Waldo said, looking at the small steamer that would take us across the bay to Oakland. From there we were to join the newly completed Pacific Railroad through the Sierra Nevada mountains, then board a coach through the fearsome Death Valley, skirting Nevada to Arizona and the Grand Canyon.

'Nothing but the best,' Cecil replied. 'I've spared no expense to make this expedition as comfortable as possible.'

'I should think so,' snorted Aunt Hilda. 'Remember we're doing you a favour.'

We disembarked after a smooth trip, arriving just in time for the train. Everything smelt of newness – new paints, new seats, new everything. This is a very democratic country, and there was no first class, which rather annoyed Aunt Hilda. There was a very good saloon car, however, and a fine dining car.

'We seem to be going in the wrong direction,' I said, as the waiter brought us a cup of tea.

California flashed past our windows. Blue skies and sunshine reigned over lush tropical plants; flowering fruit groves; neat, bright villages. Oranges bigger than cricket balls, scented almonds, figs, grapes, lime, olives. Such bounty that we in England could only dream of.

'Yes, I noticed that,' Isaac said. 'The train said Calistoga. Surely we need to go in the opposite direction?'

'Hush.' Mr Baker shot a meaningful glance at the waiter, who was hovering nearby. When the man had gone, he explained. 'It is a device to put my brother off our trail. We will take this detour and then make extra speed through the mountains.' He flushed. 'Besides, I am feeling unwell and the hot springs there can work miracle cures.'

He flashed a glance at his arm as he said this, where his illness crawled on his skin in the form of the snake. His papery face burned in my mind. His glowing eyes. I was tired. I could take no more. I rose and said I was going back to my cabin to lie down. Rachel rose to accompany me, though I really didn't want her to.

'Are you all right?' she asked as we left the dining car.

I shrugged.

'I'm really worried about you. Ever since, you know, you woke up . . . well, you haven't been quite . . .'

'Myself?'

'Yes. I suppose that's one way of putting it.'

'I'm sorry. You mustn't worry.'

'I can't help it, Kit. Is there anything I can do?'

She looked gently determined. There is more to Rachel

70

than there seems at first; she is so kind and soft people can mistake her for feeble. Aunt Hilda thinks she is a halfwit. She is wrong. Rachel is one of the most stubborn people I know. I could have told her about my dreams, the feeling of some foreign mind probing in my head. But I didn't. Rachel already had enough to worry about – besides, if I let her know what was troubling me, she would never leave it alone.

But there was a question I wanted to ask her. With my aunt and Waldo safely out of earshot, I bent low and said:

'There is something.'

'Yes?'

'It's Waldo. What's up with him? Have I offended him?'

Rachel smiled. 'I wouldn't worry about offending Waldo. His skin is thicker than a rhino's.'

'Then what have I done? Sometimes I think he positively dislikes me.'

Isaac, who had come out of the dining car after us, caught the end of our conversation and grinned. 'I wouldn't worry about that!' he said. 'Waldo's just embarrassed. The silly idiot.'

'About what?' I asked, but Rachel shot Isaac a warning glare and he clamped his mouth shut.

'What's Waldo got to be embarrassed about?' I probed Rachel. 'What's he done now? Why are you grinning like that, Isaac?' But I could get nothing out of them, just more smirking from Isaac, who really showed no sense at all.

Shortly after this, we arrived in Calistoga. We were staying at the Hot Springs Hotel, built at great cost by California's first millionaire, Sam Brannan. This rogue of a businessman had made his fortune by selling shovels to the prospectors who flocked to the land, desperate to find gold. The hotel was an enchanting sugar cube of a building which rose near the railway tracks, circled by lawns and little cottages with gingerbread gables. There was an ice rink, tennis courts, a ballroom. All this in the very middle of nowhere! The town of Calistoga itself is a small settlement with just one street, surrounded by woody hills and overhung by the grim Mount Helena.

A smell of sulphur hangs over the town, something rich and strange in the air. I felt as we entered the grounds of the hotel that this was somewhere special. The area was sacred to the Indians who lived here before the coming of the white man. They believed the geysers and hot springs had healing properties – and forbade fighting in the area.

We had a pleasant meal. I wanted an early night as we had to leave at dawn, but Mr Baker insisted we sample one of the famous mud baths. He seemed to think it would be good for my health. Aunt Hilda was all for it, but Rachel made a face and refused. She said the idea of lying up to one's neck in bubbling brown mud was 'revolting beyond belief – but you try it, Kit'. She added hastily, 'It might help you feel better.'

Waldo and Isaac also made some excuse. So I was stuck in the mud bath with Aunt Hilda, in a frilly bathing dress which made her look like a marquee, and Mr Baker. It's an odd sensation, the mix of sulphurous water, volcanic ash and peat bubbling between your fingers, sliming between your toes. Not unpleasant. Perhaps it is the natural springs that make one feel so drowsy. Looking downwards, I felt unusually detached from my body; all I could see of myself was hidden by mud, popping away like chocolate pudding in a huge vat . . . Mmm, if it only tasted as good as it felt.

I was more relaxed than I had been since I'd woken from my coma. How cowardly my friends were not to give it a try. This was . . . pleasant. Staring skywards I took in the sun sinking in a filmy scarlet ball, the birdsong, the stillness of this broad, huge valley. I scarcely listened to my aunt as she burbled on to Mr Baker about our coming journey. Then even she fell silent and closed her eyes. I was sinking into a light, pleasant doze.

When I awoke, Mr Baker was staring at me. His pale eyes were drilling into mine, his papery face flushed with the heat of the mud. He wanted something from me. It was as if he wished he could feel inside my head.

Strangely, I wasn't scared.

'What is it?' I asked.

He dropped his eyes then. He had a big muddy smear on his cheek, ridiculous in such a neat old man. In fact he looked bizarre, his head bobbing, disembodied, over the sea of brown mud. For a second I wanted to laugh, but his expression was too fearful.

'I know you want something,' I said.

'Is it that obvious?'

'What are you afraid of?'

'I don't want to scare you.'

I sighed. 'The situation could scarcely be more frightening. We're both cursed. We're both dying. We know this mission to the Grand Canyon is crazy . . . This tablet – do you even have the first idea how we're going to find it?'

He looked at me and held my gaze for a long instant. His eyes were burnt out. All I could see in them was fear, not the man he once must have been.

'Very well. You've asked . . .' he said. 'Do you feel it too?'

'Feel what?'

'Feel it. I don't know what *it* is. It *moves* in your head.'

I went rigid, every nerve tense. I had felt it, but had tried not to dwell on it. Behind my frequent headaches, there was something strange, sinister.

'Prodding, poking about in there. Like a maggot in your brain. Looking for a way to burrow in deeper—'

'What's doing this?' I interrupted. 'If you know, for heaven's sake, tell me.'

'I don't have the answers. All I have is a feeling. A very strong feeling. I think it's Cecil.'

'Your brother? But that's impossible. How could he . . .' My voice trailed off. 'How could he get in my head?'

'I told you he is a shaman. A magician. He hates me now and he has *always* hated you. He is playing with us. Playing inside our heads.'

'How can you know? I mean—'

'We're twins,' he cut in. 'Cecil and I have been together since we were babies. We lost our first tooth in the same week, courted our first girl together. Not that there's been much courting in our lives. The business always came first. Now we're wrenched apart and it's as if I've lost half my arm. Sometimes I think any hell would be better than losing my twin.'

'You've been brave to leave him.'

'Don't you see? It's just because I know him so well. In so many ways I *am* him. This is why I know it's him in my mind. I know his . . . his . . . How can I put it? . . . His handwriting.'

I glanced at Aunt Hilda. She was snoring lightly. I was shrouded in a chill fog. Me and Cyril Baker together, struggling through the murk. Everything was dark now, the momentary peace gone.

'Playing inside our heads,' I murmured.

Cyril's mouth closed with a snap. To my left Aunt Hilda grunted and opened her eyes. She flashed a suspicious look at me and then at Cyril, as if we had played some trick on her.

'It's nearly dark,' she said. 'Better wash off some of this muck and get to bed. It's an early start tomorrow.' She heaved her body out of the tub, like a great muddy whale. Mutely I followed as she waddled off across the lawn towards our lodgings.

I heard Cyril cough in the dusk behind me. Heard the slap of his feet on the path. How could he have described the feeling of something inside my head so well if it hadn't happened to him too? But that his brother was some sort of magician who could enter other people's minds . . . The idea was fantastic.

I knew, deep down, that Cyril had only told me a part of the story. All the things I didn't know cast shadows over my thoughts. I was convinced he was still hiding something. It may have been true that his twin was playing in our minds. But there was more – I *knew* it. I could only guess what Cecil was really planning: the beating heart of our mission was still secret.

✑ Chapter Nine ✑

I almost didn't see Cyril Baker waiting by the stagecoach. The man was becoming more see-through every day. As if he was shrinking, vanishing. He didn't mention our talk of the night before, but I couldn't look at him without a dark cloud descending.

There were eight horses to pull the stagecoach. They pawed at the ground, their breath rising in steaming fingers. The driver was on his seat, his whip between his legs. As well as a broad-brimmed Stetson hat, a holstered pistol and an ammunition belt jangling at his hip, there was another shotgun by his seat. The only law, as one went west, was the barrel of a gun. Indians, cowboys, miners and homesteaders fought for control of these wild lands. They would shoot first and ask questions later.

The coach, built by the famous Concord company, was very sturdy. It had two huge wheels at the back and could seat nine inside. Two more could hitch up next to the driver, and for short journeys it was known for five or six extra passengers to clamber on the roof. At the moment the roof was stacked with our suitcases and trunks. Luckily this coach was hired for our private use.

'The front seat, madam?' Mr Baker asked my aunt.

'Humph,' she grunted. 'Should think so. Waldo, you can squeeze up here too. Sit next to the driver.'

She had swatted Mr Baker aside like a fly, choosing the most comfortable seats for herself and Waldo. Cyril was finding, like most men, that my aunt is an unstoppable force. The softer emotions were not natural to my dear aunt, but I wondered briefly if she ever dwelled on her friend Mr Gaston Champlon, who had died in an avalanche in India. They were very friendly before his death, and I'd sometimes even hoped they might get married. But now it was impossible to imagine my gruff aunt ever letting a man rule her.

For the journey across the mountains Rachel, Isaac and I were stuck with Mr Baker for company. He sat across from me, knees locked uncomfortably close to mine. I was often conscious of his eyes on me. It was as if nothing else existed for him, just me and my mind. In a dark moment I even wondered if it was him who was entering my head, playing tricks with my sanity. Was this all part of some cruel game?

I thrust the thought away as soon as it entered my head. You have to trust someone in this world. Hadn't he given my friends solid proof in Chinatown of his change of heart?

The sights of the California mountains were wonderful.

Instead of our English oak and ash, they have trees such as the evergreen manzanita, the maple, the buckeye and of course the fabulous redwood. These monster trees grow higher than a church steeple, and there is one so huge they've cut a hole in it through which you can drive a wagon and eight horses. The giant redwood is somehow very American. Everything out here is simply *bigger* – Waldo, of course, would say better as well. The mountains touch the clouds, and the great plains are amazing in scale, stretching out as far as the eye can see.

America can make dear old England feel very small.

'The last time we journeyed by stagecoach we were kidnapped by you, Mr Baker,' Rachel murmured as we drove along. 'Let us hope this journey is more pleasant.'

'My brother's idea.'

'Mr Baker's presence here will provide insurance against being kidnapped, I'm sure,' I said.

He smiled uneasily at that and for many miles there was silence. Stagecoach travel in America is a bone-shaking experience. The seats are hard and you're jolted and rattled up and down till your very breath feels shaky. Dust blows in through the open window, coating everything and leaving you choking for breath. We were all delighted to stop for lunch at a curious attraction called the Petrified Forest.

This contains the stumps of huge redwoods that were

coated by volcanic ash centuries ago, weird skeletal shapes that remind you of long-dead beasts. It is managed by an enterprising Swede, who bought this land to farm. He chanced on the fossils and decided instead to turn it into a business. Now he charges fifty cents to enter the forest. Such is the spirit of America. Even old fossils can be turned into gold.

We ate our lunch of rolls, muffins, boiled eggs and ham. Well, to be honest, while the others wolfed it down, I picked. I hadn't felt properly hungry since I'd woken from my coma. Food made a sick feeling rise in my throat. I noticed Mr Baker hardly ate either. He was jumpy, starting at every noise, constantly on the lookout for his brother. Afterwards, we wandered awhile in the forest. Eerily silent, the ghosts of past trees all around, it brought home to me the immense age of America. Only Aunt Hilda seemed unaffected by the spirit of the place.

'We'd better get on, Baker,' she boomed after we'd been in the forest a mere half-hour. 'We need to be at the trading post by nightfall.'

So we were off again, keeping up the same relentless pace. Climbing the rutted track, up and up. The horses were lathered in froth before we reached the way station where we would change horses and spend the night. Not much of a place, I must admit. A wooden shack with a tin roof and another shack for the horses. Around the houses

80

was some pasture, and a vegetable patch, but the forest pressed in on all sides, deep and dark.

It looked a lonely place to live.

Waldo jumped down from his place near Aunt Hilda. He was smiling and looked fresher than the rest of us.

'At least we'll get bacon for breakfast,' he said, pointing to the pig pen near the shack.

The innkeeper came out at last to meet us. He was a small, wrinkled man in a grey apron smeared with blood. He greeted us courteously and offered refreshments, but when he saw Mr Baker his face twisted in a puzzled frown.

'Back already? What happened to your red coach? Did you smash it up?'

For a moment no one understood what he was talking about. Our coach was black, a very smart black and gold. Then the light dawned. Cyril Baker stared at him, blood draining from his already bloodless face.

'What is it, man?' the innkeeper said. 'You look like you've seen a ghost. I'm only saying you left yesterday – and now look at you. Back with a new gig. Not as fancy as the last one though.'

'That must have been my brother, Cecil,' Cyril said at last. 'People say we're very alike.'

'Alike? You're the spitting image of each other. You two playing hide-and-seek over the mountains?'

But Cyril didn't reply. Turning away, he asked for his bag

to be taken to his room, which the innkeeper's son did. So our plan to throw his brother off our scent by detouring to Calistoga had failed. Even worse, Cecil Baker was ahead of us, which meant that if we didn't make up speed he would reach the Grand Canyon before us.

Cyril had warned that if he found the tablet before we did, the consequences would be catastrophic.

That evening we partook of the most revolting meal of my life. In the inn's rough kitchen we sat round a dirty wooden table. There were barrels for chairs, no stove, just a fire with a big pot suspended above. There were no cupboards or dressers or shelves, not even a floor, just earth packed hard under our feet.

'Slumgullion,' the innkeeper said, sloshing some greyish stew into our tin cups. 'Oughtter keep you going.'

What can I say? Slumgullion is a mix of sand, bacon rind, grease, dish-rag and probably pig droppings. The others gulped it disgustedly down, along with gritty hunks of cornbread. I managed no more than one mouthful and Mr Baker had not even that.

After such a feast what could we do but retire early? There were no gas lamps in this simple shack so we took candles up to our rooms. I was sharing a mattress with Rachel while Aunt Hilda slept on the cot. Even if I had not been uneasy, my brain throbbing, my back aching on the hard floor, my aunt's snoring would have made a good night's sleep impossible. At midnight, Rachel put a pillow over her head. If anything, her snores became louder.

I finally fell into a heavy sleep around dawn. I had one of those dreams in which you feel like you've been drugged, or hit over the head with a sandbag. I knew I was sleeping, but I couldn't wake, as a very pale man in a very pale gown came up to me. He looked like a mummy, with no hands or feet but trailing yards of bandages. The man leaned over me, breathing in my face, his papery skin crackling.

It was Cyril or Cecil Baker – I couldn't tell which. His eyes drilled into my brain, and then he held out a pale hand and stroked my hair. Stroked it as if he wanted to pull it out by the handful. Then I noticed the snake on his neck, crawling up to his cheek.

'WHAT'S THE MATTER? KIT, ARE YOU ALL RIGHT?' Rachel was holding me, her face inches from mine. In the background I could see Aunt Hilda was upright, awoken suddenly from her sleep.

'Fine,' I gasped, backing away from Rachel. My face was sweaty, my hair damp. 'Just a bad dream.'

'You were screaming, child!' Aunt Hilda snapped.

'Hush, everything is just fine. No need to worry,' Rachel said. 'Shhhh,' she murmured to me, as if I was a small child. Her soothing voice stilled my heartbeat and gradually I found myself calming down.

Aunt Hilda and Rachel were both gentle with me.

Indeed, after a good bacon breakfast with the bright California sunshine streaming through the window, it was hard to believe in my night fears.

∾∾∾

After breakfast Rachel and I went to collect our bags and things. As soon as I entered our room, I knew something was wrong. Not that anything had been disarranged – but I could sense something. Rachel didn't notice anything and we packed away our nightgowns and toothbrushes and so on while she chattered on about the amazing beauty of the West. She was nervous about the trip through the desert, where nothing grew except cacti. Finally everything was ready for our departure. Except one thing.

'Have you got my hairbrush?' I asked Rachel.

'No.' She turned round and scanned the room. There was no place to hide a mouse in the dingy little chamber. Just bare wooden floorboards, a chest of drawers, a wash bowl with a cracked mirror above it.

'Have you looked in the chest of drawers?'

'Why would I put my hairbrush in a chest of drawers?' I replied. 'I left it by the washbasin. I know I did.'

I could conjure up a picture of my hairbrush. Wooden-backed, full of my tangled brown hair.

'Rachel, I brushed my hair before breakfast. I know I

did, and then I left it right there.' I pointed to the empty space by the wash bowl.

It was a mystery of the kind you will be familiar with. You lose a favourite hairclip or purse. Usually you blame imps, or borrowers, or your own absent-mindedness, but this time the disappearance of my hairbrush struck both of us as odd.

Rachel looked at the floor and stifled a small scream. There on the boards was the print of dusty shoe. A large shoe, far too large for either of us – or Aunt Hilda. I saw another footprint by the door – clearer than the first.

That settled it. Though the room was dingy, it was very clean and the floor had been mopped before our arrival. The footprint belonged to a stranger. While we had breakfasted downstairs, someone – a man, by the size of his feet – had crept up here and stolen my hairbrush.

'Who would want your grubby old hairbrush?' Rachel said. She attempted a smile. 'Unless it's Waldo, as a sort of love token.'

I blushed. 'What are you talking about?' I said. 'He can hardly stand the sight of me these days.'

'Witchcraft,' Rachel whispered. 'Witches were stealing your hair. What do they say? A lock of hair, a piece of skin, fingernail clippings. That's what witches use, isn't it? This smells of witchcraft.'

'Rubbish. All that stuff is just gibberish. Look out of the window at the mountains and that green grass and the pigs snuffling at the trough. That's what is real. All the rest is just—'

'That's what you *say*, Kit,' Rachel interrupted. 'I know what you're up to. You're keeping something from me . . . I saw how you looked a moment ago, just because your hairbrush was lost. Well, tell me that's normal.'

'It is normal,' I said. But I was lying. Nothing about this situation was normal. Not the feeling of something crawling in my head. Not the fear the missing hairbrush had stirred up in me. Not the snake, which had moved infinitesimally up my arm. I couldn't bother Rachel with all this though. Her dread would only make me feel even worse. Luckily Aunt Hilda bellowed from below that the stagecoach was waiting, so with a hurried exclamation I picked up my bags and went outside for my shoes.

But they were gone. Rachel's pair was there, outside our door. But my own sturdy brown brogues had vanished. At that moment Rachel came out of the room, and when she saw my face she looked terrified.

I rushed downstairs.

'Has anyone seen my shoes?' I asked Aunt Hilda, who was carrying her bag out of the door.

'They are outside your room.'

'No, they're not. They've disappeared.'

She sighed impatiently. 'I'll show you.'

Rachel and I trooped up the stairs after her and there, lying outside our door, just where I had left them, were my shoes. My dusty brown shoes.

Either they had vanished and then returned. Or both Rachel and I were going mad.

❧ Chapter Ten ❧

Our passage through California to Arizona should have been wonderful. Giant sequoia trees, vertical cliffs, canyons and cascading waterfalls gradually gave way to parched deserts dotted with cacti. But we were too frightened, pushed ourselves too hard, to take pleasure in the landscape. Always we seemed to go on the hardest route, down trails rutted by the men and women who had come before us, those hardy pioneers. We kept away, though, from the main stagecoach stations. Cyril Baker had been badly scared by the reported sighting of his brother. When he heard the story of the ghostly shoes, he became as jumpy as a startled deer.

I couldn't help feeling sorry for him. He was living on his nerves, hardly eating. His white skin had taken on a bluish tinge and he was so thin a breeze could blow him over. I wondered if I looked as awful as he did. Our affliction had made a strange sort of friendship between us. After a day or two of our journey, Cyril had managed to boot Waldo off the shotgun position next to the driver. Now he rode with my aunt. He said he wanted to be on the lookout. I knew he was armed, like the driver and Waldo. We were bristling with pistols, which should have made us feel safer. It didn't. The more guns there are around, the less secure you feel.

The journey became harder every day. As we left California's almond-scented climes, we saw fewer people. The occasional wary Indian, face painted with ochre. A couple of squaws, their babies tied in a bundle to their backs. Now and then a lonely rancher or wild-eyed cowboy. Sand blew in our faces, putting a burning screen before our eyes, making us gasp for air. Our throats rasped as we poured sips of warm water down them. But we had to be careful. Mr Baker had brought plenty of supplies – the explanation for the boxes on top of the stagecoach – but as we came down off the Panamint Mountains and into Death Valley water was more precious than gold.

This valley is the hottest place in America, with a sun that scorched our horses as they laboured, panting, to pull our coach. Our cowboy hats protected us from the worst of it, but the sun still bored fiery spikes into our heads. The pioneers who had travelled out here in search of riches in the gold rush had named this area Death Valley. Like us they were in a frantic hurry. I hoped we would be luckier than they were and would not lose members of our expedition to sunstroke and dehydration.

Waldo sat next to me on the ride through the valley, pressing into me and shading me from the sun coming in through the window. We were both sweating, damp with exhaustion. He paid no attention to me. Still, he seemed a little less hostile. Before we entered the desert, he had seemed to take pains to sit as far away from me as possible.

When all the others were dozing I took my opportunity to say a few words to him.

'Waldo,' I whispered, 'I've never thanked you properly for what you did for me. When I was in a coma, I mean.'

He shifted uncomfortably, trying to move his arm away from me. I noticed his face was pink, his lip beaded with sweat.

'It was nothing,' he murmured.

'I could hardly have been very good company.'

'You were more . . . relaxing . . . than usual, certainly.'

I flushed. 'That's not very kind.'

He shrugged. 'Maybe your coma knocked some sense into you.'

'What? You think I'm better off in a coma?'

'I didn't say that.'

I looked at him. His blue eyes gleamed at me through layers of sweat and grime. A lock of sun-streaked hair fell into his eyes.

'Look, Waldo, I was just trying to say thank you. Why do we have to argue? Why—'

'Why can't we just be friends?' he interrupted, finishing my sentence. 'Because friends respect each other. Friends listen to each other. You've never taken the blindest bit of notice of what I say. You always charge along in your own bullish way, and I feel, frankly, that you're not *safe*. You—'

'That's not fair,' I cut in. 'You said yourself I was quieter – look, Rachel said you sat with me all the time when I was ill. I was just trying to be polite because she said –' I stopped suddenly because I noticed that in the heat of the argument we had raised our voices. Aunt Hilda, Rachel and Isaac had woken up and were all staring at us, grinning like idiots.

'It's just like the good old days,' Isaac said. 'Waldo and Kit at daggers drawn.'

'Just a little lovers' tiff,' Aunt Hilda said. 'Take no notice.'

I bit my lip, humiliated. Waldo moved further away, which is hard to do when squeezed into a sweltering stagecoach.

'You're quite mistaken, ma'am,' he said to Aunt Hilda. 'Your niece and I can barely tolerate each other.'

I was so angry and ashamed I could hardly look at anyone. Well, here it was in black and white. Waldo could barely tolerate me. And I'd thought he was a friend, a good friend.

I'd have to try to be more formal with him in the future.

Aunt Hilda hadn't had enough of embarrassing us both:

'Stuff and nonsense, Waldo. You adore my niece. Anyone would. Stop talking guff.' She grunted. 'Look at you two. Carrying on like a couple of—'

Midway through her sentence she stopped as gunfire cut her off. One, two, three shots. Thunderclaps that reverberated deafeningly around the interior of the stagecoach. We were cantering down a steep road which was overhung by a sharp slab of reddish rock covered in pinyon pines and thorny shrubs. Now our horses lurched to a halt in a cloud of dust. The seven black mares and one tawny stallion all neighing and rocking in alarm. Our coach swayed giddily from side to side.

Peering out in front of us, I couldn't see anyone firing a gun, just the desert stretching away down below in monotonous whirls of sand. Then a man on horseback emerged from a crack in the rock. He had a coiled length of rope slung over one arm and a pistol pointing straight at Mr Baker.

'I got y'all covered,' the man boomed. 'Anyone moves and your friend gets hisself a bullet right through the neck.'

❧ Chapter Eleven ❧

'Driver!' Aunt Hilda shrieked. 'Shoot him.'

A flour sack covered the rider's face, with holes cut out for his eyes.

'Don't try anything,' he said. Lazily he waved his gun towards some bushes. 'My men have got you pegged out and hung up to dry.'

Glinting from the bushes were the barrels of other guns. One, two, three, four . . . I counted at least five. One of the unseen bandits let out a warning volley, which whistled over our heads and exploded harmlessly in the desert.

'Now y'all get out the coach. Fast – before my men peg you full of holes.'

'Driver!' Hilda shrieked again as we clambered out of the coach and lined up at its side. 'Waldo! Do something!'

'Calm down, Aunt Hilda,' I hissed. My heart was hammering, my hands clammy. 'If we give them our money, they'll leave us alone.'

The driver wasn't putting up any manner of fight. He

was dismounting, his hands held over his head. The bandit threw him a coil of the rope he was wearing.

'Tie that guy up,' he ordered, pointing to Baker. 'Hands together real tight.'

The driver tied Baker's hands together and shoved him down the track at the side of the road.

'Faster!' the masked outlaw urged Baker. 'Quit stallin'. Ain't no lawman gonna save your sorry soul.'

While the bandit's attention was distracted, Waldo slid his pistol, a nickel-plated Colt 54, small but lethal, out of its holster and slipped it into his left boot. He did it in one swift movement, turning away from the outlaws in the bushes. I don't think anyone noticed except me.

Then he pressed against me for a moment. He breathed in my ear: 'If you get a chance, distract them.'

With Baker tied up, the outlaw turned his attention to the rest of us. He jumped off his horse and, shooing the shaking driver in front of him, came round to the stagecoach. I noticed the duster coat he wore, made of sand-coloured linen, was tattered and had several patches. Close up his stovepipe hat was worn. He walked up and down inspecting us as we stood alongside the coach. Finally he came to a stop. His eyes were on Rachel, following her through the holes in the sack.

'You ever been to Dodge City?' he asked her

'I'm English.'

'I saw this singer there, looked just like you.' The outlaw let out a low whistle and his gun barrel skimmed Rachel's hair. 'Why, I believe a pretty little gal like you could have a mighty fine time in Dodge.'

Rachel drew closer to me.

My thoughts were racing. If this gang intended to harm Rachel, it would be better to take our chances right now. I glanced at Waldo and he nodded. I planned to cause a diversion, faint on the outlaw, groaning theatrically and using his body as cover. Perhaps we could get Waldo's pistol on him before his men in the bushes started shooting. But the outlaw was too quick. Noticing Waldo's empty holster hanging off his belt, he grabbed him by the collar. If I made a mistake now, he would blow Waldo's head off.

'Where's your gun, sonny?' His voice was muffled through the sack.

'I lost it.'

'Bull – you ain't lost nothin'.' He twisted Waldo's shirt in his hand, making him squirm. Then he shook him off.

'Take off them boots!' he said, waving his gun.

'Who, me?' Waldo said.

'Yep, you, Johnny Englishman.'

'I'm more American than you,' Waldo protested. 'I'm an honest—'

'Cut it. Don't make no difference – take 'em off.'

Waldo did as he was told.

'Turn 'em upside down and shake 'em,' the outlaw ordered.

Waldo shook his boots. His pistol fell out, thudding onto the sand. The outlaw bent forward to pick it up. Now was Waldo's chance. He could kick the thug in the head. But I was forgetting the other members of the gang, hidden in the bushes. They were awfully quiet, I thought suddenly, those other outlaws. Quiet and almost invisible, except for the glint of the silver gun barrels.

Waldo disposed of, the bandit in the stupid flour sack was taking his time. Now he was whistling through his teeth as he stripped us down. One by one he patted us for weapons, lingering over Rachel, and then made us all line up by the side of the road. He stripped us of all our valuables: coins, watches, Cyril's gold pillbox ring, Aunt Hilda's mannish signet ring, which had belonged to my grandfather. All that was most precious to us. I watched him take my mother's locket. It would mean nothing to him.

Now the outlaw made the driver go through our things in the stagecoach. The two of them stripped us of everything. The pouch of gold pieces Mr Baker had hidden in one of the trunks, our store of dollars, food, best clothes.

Waldo was made at gunpoint to give up the fine gold watch that had belonged to his father, which he had hidden at the bottom of his trunk. At that I felt sick and Rachel gasped, but Waldo said nothing. I knew how he loved that watch. His father had died years ago, when Waldo was a little boy. He couldn't remember him at all – that watch was the only thing he had of his. But the thug didn't care. He was working fast now, shovelling our booty into the leather saddlebags on his horse. He threw out another set of bags, which he made us fill.

'Hey, Mr Flour Sack,' I said, 'why do the other guys leave all the hard work to you?'

Through the sack, the bandit began to chuckle. He turned to his comrades in the bushes. 'Hear that, Jesse? This young lady thinks I'm doin' the sweatin' here.'

While he talked, the outlaw made the driver unhitch the reins so that all the horses were let loose. All except one, the handsome stallion. The bandit slapped the mares on the rumps and fired a couple of shots in the air, which made them canter down the track, disappearing round the bend in a haze of dust.

Our horses were gone.

Then he mounted his own horse and motioned the driver to mount the stallion, a tawny beauty with powerful forelegs and a foaming mane. I looked at the driver, my suspicions mounting. The man hadn't said a word during the entire hold-up. He was meant to protect us, but he hadn't done a single darn thing.

'I'm taking your man with me as a hostage,' the outlaw said. 'You wait here for half an hour before you move.'

'You've let our all horses go,' Aunt Hilda grunted. 'How precisely will we go anywhere?'

'Don't you English dames ever shuddup? Like I said, one step outta line and my men will get you.' He pointed to the gun barrels, and then he was gone, riding that trail into the bushes, herding the driver before him.

Waldo sat down on the track, letting out a heavy groan. Slowly he began to put his boots back on. He had only been standing on the sand for a few minutes, but already his feet were burnt raw. His movements were halting, I noticed. Waldo is always a bit clumsy. He lost his little finger in India to frostbite and would have not been so clever with a gun if Isaac hadn't made him an artificial finger.

I sat down next to him. The sand was burning through my cotton travelling skirt. Everything around us was desolate, no creature alive within sight except a single dark vulture wheeling in the burning sky. Above us was the slab of red rock covered in thorny bushes and down below the Mojave Desert. Mile after mile of hot sand with nothing growing but those strange contorted cacti. Little hope of rescue, for no one, not even the toughest pioneers, lived in these parts.

'I guess we'll never know,' Waldo said, looking towards

the haze of dust, which was all that there was left of the outlaw and our driver.

'Know what?' Isaac asked.

'Whether that driver was in league with the outlaws?'

'Oh – I'm pretty sure he was,' Isaac said. 'I mean he didn't exactly *do* anything, did he? And he was supposed to be this big, tough cowboy hero . . . Anyway, one thing's for sure.'

'What's that?' Aunt Hilda snapped.

'We're never going to see them again. Not the driver, not the outlaw and least of all our money.'

❧ Chapter Twelve ❧

Mr Baker coughed apologetically, holding his hands out in front of him. They were still firmly tied, the string cutting into his wrists.

'This is rather uncomfortable,' he said.

Waldo moved over. A knife would have cut through, but the bandit had taken all our weapons. It was a struggle to untangle them and in the end he had to use his teeth to bite through a particularly stubborn knot. The outlaws hadn't left us anything with which to cut the string, not even a pocket knife.

'Well, I guess that we should gather anything we've got left to eat and get moving,' I said. Our stagecoach was useless now, a hulking black thing, burning in the sun.

'What about the other bandits?' Rachel pointed to the bushes, where the rifle barrels still glinted. 'They're watching.'

'Haven't you realised?' I asked.

'So you cottoned on.' Isaac grinned.

'What . . . are you talking about?' the others chorused.

'They aren't real,' I said, pointing to the glinting barrels.

We turned to look at the bushes, dotted with five gun barrels all trained on us. Five gun barrels that hadn't moved an inch during the entire hold-up. Five outlaws who hadn't showed their faces in support of their leader.

'Real outlaws don't just sit in the bushes,' Isaac said. 'Surely you noticed.'

Waldo was fuming, his face red with anger. 'If you two are so clever, why didn't you tell the rest of us? . . . Darn it,' he began to shout. 'If I had known there was only one man with a gun, I WOULDN'T HAVE LET HIM TREAT ME LIKE AN IDIOT. I WOULD HAVE KILLED HIM—'

'Calm down, Waldo,' I cut in, raising my voice above his. 'I only realised too late.'

Aunt Hilda, who shared Waldo's loud indignation, was marching up to the bushes behind him. The rest of us followed. We went up to the gap between the pinyon pines through which the outlaw had appeared. A lizard scuttled out of my way. It was easy to spot where a path had been forced into the shrubbery.

There, in and behind the bushes, we found the rest of the 'outlaws' and their 'guns'. Five bottles rigged up on a system of twigs and string. Five bottles, their silver-painted necks sparkling in the sun, looking just like gun barrels.

Isaac began to laugh – and I couldn't help joining him. It

really was a neat little ruse. 'Really ingenious that outlaw,' Isaac said. 'He had me fooled for a—'

'Ten seconds?' Aunt Hilda barked. 'Next time share your insights with us, Israel.'

Isaac giggled, but a look at our glum faces and the dawning realisation of the hole we were in made him stop, fast. We really were stuck. In front of us was desert, behind us was desert, and to the side was arid rock. All that grew here were tough plants, like the bulbous Joshua tree. They dropped their roots deep into the sand, searching for every drop of water. Like the desert fox and the lizard, they had learned to survive. But with the sun beating down on our heads, and the scorching sand reflecting the heat back up, *we* wouldn't last long.

'How much water do we have left?' Aunt Hilda asked.

Isaac was scrabbling in the trunk that held the food – the measly bits the bandits had left us. His face as he turned to us was grave.

'Just two canisters,' he said. 'That'll last the six of us a couple of days at the most.'

I looked at the horizon, towards the end of Death Valley. There was a blue smudge visible. Hope, water, a town or homestead and our salvation. But, tramping on our own two feet under that merciless sun, it would take a lot more than a couple of days to reach it.

❧ Chapter Thirteen ❧

By the second day of walking my feet had become separated from my body. They marched on of their own accord, while my head floated somewhere in the cloudless sky. By my side Aunt Hilda groaned, her cheeks flaming in the shade of her cowboy hat. I rarely glanced at Waldo, who was all grim concentration as he plodded on in his leather boots. The desert stretched ahead of us and all around: whorls of sand, barren mountains and those endless shifting dunes. It was bare of all but the most scrubby plants.

I had travelled through an endless desert before, in Egypt. I knew firsthand what it was like: the searing heat; the sand that chokes the back of your throat, creeps into your nose and ears, makes the very act of breathing a painful battle against dust. But in our last voyage through the desert we'd ridden camels and carried provisions. Above all, we'd had water.

Now we walked and walked and walked. With each step the way became harder on our legs and our hearts.

Our water was severely rationed. Waldo had been

elected to carry it and gave us just a sip at a time. Enough to wet our parched lips, and moisten the back of our throats. Not enough to have an actual drink. Not enough to feel the sweet liquid glug down your throat and soothe the fire in your gut. Not enough to quell the raging thirst that consumed me.

Have you ever been thirsty before? Really thirsty, dying of thirst?

If the answer is yes, you will know how it is. All you can think of is water. Our vitally important mission to the Grand Canyon to find the tablet that would save our lives and thwart Cyril's evil twin did not cross my mind. I had almost forgotten what we were doing here; our desperate journey was obscured by burning sand. All I thought of was a trickle of cool water gurgling down my gullet.

'Is it the same for you?' Cyril asked towards evening on the second day as he stumbled on beside me. The burning sun was sinking below the horizon. Falling in the bleached sky, veiled by a shimmering haze of white. A land of white sun.

'What?' I asked, licking a trickle of sweat off my upper lip. 'Wanting water?'

I glanced at him with dislike. I had almost forgotten he had sacrificed his wealth for this journey. I saw only a strange, pale creature, his ghastly eyes popping out of his head. Unlike the rest of us, he hadn't been roasted raw by the sun. Rather, it had seemed to bake all the juices from his body, leaving it a shrivelled white husk.

'No, not that. The other thing. Don't you feel it?'

'Feel what?' I said, a bit impatiently. Words wasted energy and made our throats feel even more sore, like sandpaper.

'I think my brother has left my mind.'

I stared at him for a moment, then turned my head to peer forward. Was that something, just the faintest shine of cool blue on the desert floor? Water. Water. Please let it be water.

'Did you hear me, Kit? Cecil has left my head. Is it the same for you?'

'Ye-es. Maybe. Yes . . .' Now that he mentioned it, I hadn't felt that uneasy sense of something crawling in my head recently. Wriggling, squirming. It was too hot to feel anything, however.

'We've been set free,' Cyril went on. 'I don't know why, but think what this means. Perhaps we've given him the slip. We're winning somehow.'

'Maybe he's just resting,' I replied. But I wasn't really listening. I hadn't ever really been convinced that Cecil Baker was inside my mind. How was that possible? Besides, over there in front of us, the blue thing. Yes, that was water. It *had* to be water.

'Water!' I rasped.

'What?' Cyril's head snapped forward, his brother

temporarily forgotten. He scanned the desert. But by now others had seen the lake.

'Water!' Waldo shouted. 'Water!'

'It may be a mirage,' Aunt Hilda warned. But hope stirred in our hearts. We ran as fast as our weak legs could carry us towards the great flat basin where water shimmered. A haze of blue, dancing with light. What an exquisite sight. A thing to gladden the heart. A shallow lake, surrounded by jagged white cracks in the desert floor.

I had never seen anything more beautiful.

My heart turned over as I saw Rachel running after Waldo, a mad gleam in her eye. Her usually glossy chestnut hair was dried out by the sun and hung in dirty, brittle ropes. Her skin was burnt and cracked. Yet still she had the energy to run.

I must have stopped for a moment, because Isaac was by my side. His glasses were misted, his eyes grave as he looked into mine.

'Don't give up now, Kit. Just a few more minutes.'

'I'm fine,' I replied. 'Don't worry. I'll make it.'

'Here,' he said, offering an arm.

I almost wanted to laugh. Isaac, with his glasses and his lanky uncoordinated limbs, was weaker than I am in most normal circumstances. But now, for me, the world was shimmering, the lake moving up and down. For a second the sky went black, and when I looked at Isaac I saw nothing. I looked again and saw him standing there, holding out his hand. He looked as weary as Rachel, his eyes hectic and red patches on his cheeks. He was at the end of his tether, yet still he was trying to help me.

'Thank you,' I whispered, as I took his arm.

Waldo had turned round, on the edge of the lake, to see what the problem was. When he saw me leaning against Isaac and hobbling towards the lake, he smiled, sort of, and turned away again. I really didn't think I could make those last few steps to the lake – but somehow I did.

'Not a mirage,' Aunt Hilda shouted joyfully, kneeling down at the water's edge, dipping her fingers in. 'A real lake. Praise heaven. Praise everything! We are saved!'

I had a moment to think it wasn't much of a lake. The water was muddy and brown-looking. But still so cool, so real, so heaven sent.

Aunt Hilda, Waldo, Rachel, Isaac and Mr Baker were all cupping their hands, using them to scoop up handfuls of the water. One by one they brought them to their lips. For some reason, though all I had thought of was water, I hung back, watching.

'Phhoooo!' Aunt Hilda spat out a mouthful of the water, which arced over Mr Baker and hit Waldo in the chest. 'Disgusting!'

One by one my friends were spitting out the water. I looked at them in wonder. It certainly looked a bit brackish and brown, but water is water. When it is going to save your life, it doesn't matter how clean it is.

'Salt!' explained Aunt Hilda. 'It's a salt lake.'

Waldo was swearing, while Mr Baker had simply collapsed.

'Shouldn't we drink it anyway?' I took a drop of water in my hand and licked. It had the briny tang of seawater.

'No!' yelped Aunt Hilda. 'It will only make things worse. The salt in the water dries out your body quicker – which means you die quicker, you dolt!'

'You don't have to abuse me,' I said, sinking on to the dry sand. I understood what had made the layers of white cracks, radiating away from us. They were caused by the salt in the drying earth. Beautiful, like a layer of paper snowflakes laid over the desert. But for us they spelled defeat.

I looked at Aunt Hilda, who was towering over me. A single tear welled up in her right eye and dropped down her cheek. She was crying. I couldn't remember her ever crying before.

'We *will* make it,' I said softly.

'How?' She sank down on her legs beside me. 'We should never have come through this place. Never. It's called Death Valley, for heaven's sake. But, no, I was stupid. I thought it was a short cut. It would save us time.'

'It wasn't your fault,' Cyril said. 'I was the one – I

couldn't wait. I didn't have much time left anyway and this route seemed the quickest—'

'We all know that you're dying, Mr Baker,' Isaac cut in. 'Doesn't seem fair that the rest of us have to join you.'

Waldo coughed. Like the rest of us he was squatting on the sand, the precious water canisters hanging from strings around his neck. All our eyes turned to look at him. All the water we had in the world. A dribble in one bottle and the other totally empty.

'No sense in going over the past. No sense in squabbling,' he said quietly. 'It wastes precious energy. Only way we're going to get out of this is if we save all our energy—'

'Stop!' Aunt Hilda's tears were all gone. A new determination blazed forth from her. 'I have the answer! A desperate measure, but it will save us.'

'I'll do anything!' Rachel said.

'We must drink our own urine,' Aunt Hilda announced.

'Urgh!' Rachel said. 'Anything but that.'

'Revolting idea,' Mr Baker muttered, shuddering.

'It is the only way,' Aunt Hilda said. 'I believe Mr Livingstone tried it in Africa when he was stuck somewhere. Or was it Lady Hester Stanhope? Urine is said to be quite nutritious.'

Radiating determination, she strode up to Waldo and held out her hand. 'The bottle, please, young Waldo. I feel the call of nature.'

'You can't be serious,' I said. Waldo was hanging on to the empty bottle, showing no sign of giving it to Hilda.

'This is it,' she said, her outstretched hand trembling slightly. 'If drinking my own . . . er . . . water . . . is the difference between living and dying, I'll do it . . . I'd go even further, I would—' Thankfully she stopped before we learned what she would do, because Waldo interrupted.

'Hilda is right,' he announced, finally giving her the bottle. 'If we don't take in some liquid, we'll die. The life is being slowly sucked out of our bodies by the sun and the heat coming from the sand. I saw you, Kit.' His eyes flashed at me, blue and angry. 'You were close to blacking out. I'm not going to let that happen.'

Mr Baker and Rachel were holding back, their faces rigid with horror. It sounded awful, drinking your own urine, but I think I was ready to do it. To close my eyes and – well, I was so light-headed already I think I could stomach any taste. This journey was my fault; I couldn't let everybody die.

'I agree with Hilda,' I said softly. 'We *have* to do this.'

Isaac began to laugh. He ran his hands through his hair and his face crumpled with something between laughter and tears.

'It's not funny,' Waldo said.

'I know, I know. I don't know why I've been so darn stupid. It must be the heat or something.'

'What?'

'We don't need to drink our urine,' Isaac explained. 'We've got all the water we need here.' His hands gestured towards the lake.

'It's salt, you fool –' Waldo began, then stopped, and a smile spread over his face. 'Can we, do you think?'

'All we need is to turn this salt water into drinking water. We need to desalinate it.'

'Bravo! Israel, you're a genius,' Aunt Hilda said. 'You can boil the salt away, can't you?' Then she paused, her face falling. 'You foolish, foolish boy, raising our hopes for nothing. We don't have a cooking pot. How can we de-sal-i-what's-it the water without a cooking pot? You should think before you raise all our hopes, you—'

'Whoa. Calm down.' Isaac raised his hand, as if soothing a snapping dog. 'I've thought of a way.'

⁓◌⁓

We drank our last water, each person receiving just enough to wet the tongue and the back of the throat. We followed Isaac's instructions carefully, digging two small pits in the sand. Using our bottles we filled the pits up with salt water from the Badwater Basin. Then we put our bottles in the water, with the tops up. We covered the pits with strips from Waldo's waterproof coat. Finally we weighted down the covering with a pebble, placed exactly above each bottle's spout.

Then we prayed.

If Isaac was right, the natural heat in the sand, which was boiling hot, would cause the water to evaporate and collect in droplets on the waterproof-coat covering above, leaving the salt behind on the sand. The droplets of clean water would run down the covering towards the pebble placed above the spout and drip into the bottle.

Isaac is very often clever about things I have no understanding of at all. We all hoped that this was one of those times he would be right. While we waited, time ticked on, the sun sinking under the horizon and shadows lengthening around us. I heard the howl of prowling wolves, or perhaps coyotes. At one stage Isaac lifted the cloth. A puff of vapour rose in the darkness.

Waldo had disappeared to see if he could find anything edible around the lake. We still had a few strips of the dried meat pounded with berries called pemmican, which is a staple food of American pioneers. The bandit, who had so callously left us to expire in the heat of the desert, had at least left us a few strips of this. Probably because he couldn't stomach it himself. Horrible tasting, like eating pieces of old shoe leather, but it had saved our lives.

Time passed, and then with an excited cry Isaac held up one of the metal water canteens.

'Ladies first,' he said, and handed the bottle to me. I smiled at Isaac and then passed it to my aunt.

She didn't stand on ceremony. She tipped her head back and drank from the bottle. Then, soon, it was my turn. I drank. There was not too much, just a dribble, enough to wet my mouth and keep away the worst of the thirst. It was warm and brackish, with a taste of roots and sand. Never mind. It was delicious. Life-giving.

Waldo had returned with a few roots and berries, which he pronounced edible. I believe one of them was called mesquite. We sat, huddled in a circle, and ate and drank. The leathery pemmican. The odd, tangy berries and roots. Our voices rang low in the desert, set against the call of wild things in the dark. There was life here, slithering things that hunted at night. The rattlesnake, the coyote, the road-runner. The magnificent golden eagle that soared far above. We were each other's protection, so we sat tight together, lighting a fire not for heat but for safety.

I thought of other feasts I'd had. Magnificent seven-course dinners. Trifle. Chocolate cake. Those sweet-sour Chinese dumplings. Apple pie and normal things like hot toast. The butter dripping into the crunchy bread. Nothing could compete with the joy of that simple meal in the desert, that tough old meat eaten with a few mashed berries and washed down with gritty water.

I was happy that night with my friends so near. Confident we would survive. We would distil more water and fill our canisters with at least enough to keep going. We would eat roots and berries. We would make it out of the desert and reach our goal of the Grand Canyon. That was when darkness descended in my mind, for who knew what we would find there?

❧ Chapter Fourteen ❧

Something was digging into me as my dream slipped away. Hoarse voices, gunfire and screams. Rachel was screaming, Isaac was screaming, Cyril was screaming. Blearily I opened my eyes and saw a face looming over me.

A stranger's face, his gun digging into my shoulder.

It belonged to a boy, maybe sixteen years old, with a piece of scarlet calico wound round his head. Long black hair framed a strong, tanned face, with high cheekbones and deep-set eyes. In the light of the stars they appeared very dark.

He was looking at me as if *he* was frightened. But he was the one standing over me with a gun pointed at my chest.

'Apaches,' Waldo whispered in my ear. 'God help us.'

The boy was still looking at me. Not at me, exactly. At my body. I jerked up, crossing my bare arms.

'What do you want?' I asked.

He couldn't understand me, for not a flicker crossed his face. He continued to gape at me, as if he had never seen a white girl before. Then he turned round and called out. Our fire had died to a few embers, but there was enough starlight to see that we were totally surrounded.

The circle we had made last night as we curled up to sleep had been ringed by a group of Indians on horseback. There were four or five men and a few young boys dressed in flowing robes and ponchos made of woven cloth and dyed deerskins. Some wore porcupine quills or feathers as decoration. Others wore cowboy hats or strips of dyed cloth round their long hair. One man had a buckskin hat decorated with eagle feathers. They trotted around us on their fine horses and grunted to each other in a hoarse tongue.

'They'll scalp us,' Mr Baker said.

I hushed him because they were watching us, and who knew what they could understand. The man in the buckskin hat was talking to the first boy, who was gesturing to me. The words flew fast in their strange, guttural language. As they were talking, I tried to remember what I had heard about Apaches, if indeed this was an Apache band. They were meant to be fierce, ruthless warriors. While many other tribes had been defeated by the white settlers and government soldiers, groups of Apaches held out under the leadership of a great brave called Geronimo. So far the government in Washington had not been able to capture him.

I'd had an argument just a few days ago with Waldo about it. He had called Indians savages, and said they should all be rounded up and placed on reservations – if not killed outright. My mind was more confused. Indians had lived in America for centuries before the coming of the white man. They had roamed the plains, lived in their tent-like tepees, tended buffalo, worshipped their gods of the stars and the earth. Did not the land belong to them?

Waldo had become heated and said I had no idea what I was talking about. He said something about 'manifest destiny' – which apparently meant that the white man was fated to rule this land. 'They fight with bows and arrows and we fight with cannon,' he said, which was true enough. It didn't make it right, though, did it? Were the settlers not stealing their land? 'You can't stop progress,' he'd said. 'The gun will always win against the spear.' Perhaps because he was so stubborn, I took the opposite view. In the end he'd called me a nincompoop and turned aside. This was before he had stopped talking to me altogether.

Now as these wild men on their horses circled us round the dying campfire it was hard to believe in my own fine words. They looked wild and smelt of blood. They would kill us without mercy. It was clear that civilised notions of pity were unknown to them.

We sat silent while they talked. What could we do? We had no guns or knives. The Apaches were arguing amongst themselves. After a while one of them, the man in the feathered buckskin hat, seemed to come to a decision. He called out to the others, and one by one they hauled us to our feet. I thought they would make us walk, but instead each of us was jerked behind a man on one of the horses.

I sat behind the boy. I was weak. Hunger, thirst and sickness were causing me to separate from my body. My head was floating. It felt like a dream, sitting bareback on that strong horse, shivering in the night chill, the boy inches away from me, guiding his animal through the starlit night. We galloped through the desert, the horse sure-footed. As we raced, the Apaches sang, a cruel wind-blown song. A song, unmistakably, of war.

When I did come back to my body, I took comfort from the horse, its warm limbs working under me. It was odd. I sensed that the boy rider in front of me was more scared of me than I was of him. But why? I was the captive here. The boy made sure to keep his flesh well away from me, had given me a rein to grip. He shuddered at the sight of me, as if I was some demon rather than a normal girl.

Incredible as it sounds, riding through the night I fell asleep. Or maybe I blacked out. I know not which. All I knew was that one minute I was there in the desert. Nothing around except that great animal's loping limbs, the murmuring song of the Apache band and the wind whistling past my ears. The next thing I knew I was waking up in some sort of dwelling. I had been stripped of my clothes and was dressed in an embroidered buckskin dress with fringes. A strip of red calico had been bound round my head. Wherever we were, it was no longer the desert as the air was fresh and cool. I was covered with stinking animal skins, around me other bundles of bedding. It was morning. I could see sunshine flooding through gaps in the roof and the walls, which were made of twigs and grass. I guessed I was in an Apache home, a shelter made of twigs and brush called a wickiup.

I saw no sign of my friends and could hear nothing. No talking. No Aunt Hilda snoring or Rachel murmuring soothing nothings. I didn't even know if they were still alive. I didn't know anything except that I was alone.

Alone with these merciless Apaches.

❧ Chapter Fifteen ❧

A few minutes later someone put their face through a hole in the wickiup. It was a girl of about my age. I had the fleeting impression of brown skin and glossy black hair. Eyes that flickered about, searching for something. Our gazes met for an instant. I saw her terror. Then she vanished.

My captors were frightened of me. Frightened beyond reason. Why? I was a sick girl, without weapon. It made no sense.

As I sat up, the bundle of cloth next to me began to move. Straw-coloured hair emerged from below the bedding. Relief flooded me. Waldo was here. Waldo. Then I saw it was Cyril Baker and disappointment nearly choked me. The old man was blinking, his beetle eyes looking around dully.

'Where are we?' I asked.

'Kit?'

'Of course I'm Kit. Where are the others?'

'They separated us.'

'That's obvious. Why? What's going on?'

He didn't answer but shook his head, looking around with the same veiled gaze. Something had gone out of him. He looked stupid as an ox.

'What's the matter? Did they hurt you? Torture you?'

He shook his head. 'When we came here, I wouldn't get off the horse.'

'What? Why?'

'I thought they were going to kill me.'

'You're not making sense.'

'They hit me over the head with a stick. I think I must have been stunned. That's the last thing I remember.'

'Never mind about that. Where are the others? My friends. What about my friends?'

'I don't know.'

'Cyril, you must gather your wits,' I said slowly. 'I know we are both sick – but if we are not clever we will die here. These savages will put us to death.'

'I am dying anyway.'

'Enough stupid self-pity. You can save yourself. You can help save me. Be a man, not a chick—'

'They think we are witches,' he interrupted.

'Witches! Witches? But that's ridiculous. Maybe they think all white men are witches.'

He sat up and the blankets fell from him. I saw that he was dressed as I was, in a loose garment made from deerskin. If it wasn't such a desperate situation, I would have laughed. He looked comical, that usually elegant man in the robes of a wild Indian.

'They do not suspect all white men, Kit. Just you and me.'

'Why?' Then suspicion struck. 'How do you know?'

'I heard them talking. They think we are bewitched. Or witches. I do not understand everything they say. The meaning is clear. We are unclean. To be put to death. That's why I didn't get off my horse.'

Something about this struck me as odd. I looked at Mr Baker hard.

'You're telling me you speak *Apache*?' The notion was unbelievable.

'Of course not. They were talking Spanish to your aunt. She was maddened, I can tell you, Kit. Thank goodness I have a few words of the language. At least I know what they believe. At least we can prepare ourselves.'

I sat very still. I could hear more now from the world outside the wickiup. Birdsong, the trickle of running water. People were moving out there. Apaches who hated us and, possibly worse, feared us. I heard voices, nearer now.

Finally I asked, 'Why us? Why you and me?'

His pale eyes looked at me scornfully. Now it was my turn to be slow.

'Don't you know? Don't you understand anything?'

I shook my head, though I think I knew what he was

going to say. But he didn't talk, simply held out his arm and the deerskin gown fell loose. I saw the snake had moved and my heart contracted. I hadn't looked at my own brand for several days. Somehow, if I didn't look, I could put it out of my mind. Now I saw my own snake had moved over my elbow. Its head had turned the other way, towards my heart. For some time I gazed at the repellent thing, too upset to think.

'The boy who captured you, he saw the brand of the snake on your arm,' Mr Baker said. 'They searched us all for a similar mark and found one on me. You and I. We are condemned, Kit. Prepare yourself. They have gone to fetch the—'

Before he could finish, two men burst into the wickiup, hollering and shouting. They were strong-limbed and each over six feet tall. I would have called them handsome, for they had fine faces, if it wasn't for their wild air. They were both wearing hide gloves. One of them seized me by the arm and pulled me out into the open, treating me so roughly that my arm was half wrenched out of its socket. Through the pain I saw mountains, slabs of red rock, greenery, a broad stream and the thatched shelters that looked so like hairy heads. The air was fresh, mountain-clear. We must be high up, in some hidden Apache place. Indians swarmed, hair greasy, their faces smeared with ochre and daubed with war paint.

Aunt Hilda was sitting in front of a smoking fire, her hands tied behind her. By her side were Rachel, Isaac and Waldo, all of them bound hand and foot. My captor prodded me towards the fire. It was the barrel of a gun in my back. Waldo had been wrong. As I had realised last night, these Apaches had guns as well as bows and arrows. I saw a sawn-off shotgun, a Winchester rifle and a Colt as well as a couple of ancient carbines. They might be 'savages', as Waldo called them, but they were savages who knew how to use nineteenth-century weapons.

Cyril stumbled by my side, a shotgun urging him on. I remembered his unfinished words and called out to him:

'You said they were sending for someone. Who? Who are they sending for?'

'The medicine man.'

'What is a medicine man?'

'Not a doctor, obviously. A medicine man is a shaman. A priest.' He glanced at me quickly, then looked away. 'We are on trial – for our lives.'

❧ Chapter Sixteen ❧

Waldo heard my exclamation and turned round, struggling to move with his bound hands and feet. When he saw me, relief flooded his face. I knew then that, whatever he said, he did not hate me. He did *care*.

For a fleeting second I forgot the guns bristling in this hidden clearing. I even forgot that I was about to be tried as a witch. I smiled at Waldo and he smiled back, and then I blushed, stupidly. A new determination gripped me. We *would* get through this.

I made my way to sit by Waldo, but the Indian prodded me in the other direction towards Aunt Hilda. I tried to ignore him, but he had a gun and was using it to poke me, so in the end I gave up and sank down on the log beside her. The Apache tied my hands tight behind my back, and bound my feet. Then, with a grunted word, he left. When he'd gone, my aunt gave me an affectionate grimace.

'Thought I'd seen the last of you.'

'I don't give up that easy.'

A lopsided smile on her pug-dog face. 'No niece of mine is a quitter.'

This was the closest that Aunt Hilda had ever come to declaring her love for me.

'I've learned from the best,' I said, and meant it.

By my side, Cyril was not doing so well. Vivid splotches of red stood out on his deathly skin. His breathing was hoarse.

'Cyril,' I whispered to Aunt Hilda. 'We need to do something.'

'What do you suggest? I dance the fandango?'

Rachel and Waldo and Isaac were all talking to me at the same time, asking questions, probing. I ignored them and replied to Aunt Hilda:

'He needs a doctor.'

'Not likely here, is it?'

I looked around helplessly. There were half a dozen wickiups in the camp, which was in a small clearing. Around us were red slabs of rock, thorny junipers and pinyon pines. We were in their stronghold, far away from the world of doctors and medicine. The English type of medicine anyway, not the Apache medicine of ghosts and herbs.

There was something wrong among the Apaches; you could tell that by the mutters, the downcast faces. Several of the women had black clay or soot smeared over their faces. The grim sky was matched by the dark mood all around. I did not think it was just *my* mood, but I could not be sure. Of course, you would feel dreary if you were branded a witch.

We sat there, ignored, for a long time, maybe one or two hours. The life of the Apache camp went on and I tried to watch and understand. Knowledge is strength; if we knew our enemy it would be easier to escape. I saw the women engaged in various tasks such as sorting nuts and berries. They pounded seeds on a big flat stone into a sort of flour, which they mixed with water into a paste and dried in the sun. Everyone was very careful to avoid us, especially Cyril Baker and me. They didn't let their eyes dwell on me for more than a second before they flickered hurriedly away. Nor did anyone come close enough to touch me, or even for my breath to touch them.

That was fine by me. I had no love for them. I thought back to my earlier words to Waldo, when I had defended the Apaches' right to America. I had argued that these wild men had more right to the land than civilised Americans, who had travelled from European countries like England and Italy and Holland to settle in this vast land. I had been an idealistic fool. I realised now that my fine words about the Indians had been naive.

An expectancy hung over the camp, as well as a gloom. We were waiting for something – probably the medicine man who would pronounce sentence on us. Once or twice I thought Waldo was trying to say something to me, over Aunt Hilda's head, with Rachel watching. His eyes had a pleading look, as if he was trying to say sorry. After a long period we were given some lunch, a tuberous root, a bit like a sweet potato, along with some mashed floury substance. It was food and we needed our strength to survive, so I ate. It was a little better-tasting than slumgullion. I gulped down some clear spring water with it. Then we were left to ourselves for many more hours. I felt weak, not with hunger and fear, but with the awareness that the prickling feeling in my head, which had dimmed in the desert, had returned with food and water. It really felt like something crawling, examining my thoughts. I would think something, then be infected by a wave of unease. Was someone watching me? Could they see into my mind?

I tried to distract myself by watching some boys of about fourteen playing together. The youths were lithe and strong, their flowing hair bound with crimson calico. They were burning something on their arms. A trial of strength, at which some screamed and flinched and others kept silent. Then someone noticed me watching and there were shouts of outrage. The party of boys vanished. More tedious hours followed, empty of everything but fear, and then finally the sun sank and a low wailing erupted from different parts of the camp.

It was an eerie song. I had never heard anything like it before. Though I knew it was human, it sounded like the keening of wild animals, like wolves or coyotes howling through the mesa. I feared it was for me, that these Apaches were chanting me and Mr Baker to our graves.

I could smell smoke too. Not in front of us, from the tangy juniper fire, but something dry burning.

'It's the wickiups,' Aunt Hilda whispered to me. 'God help us, they're burning their homes.'

Turning a little I could see two of the hairy dwellings blazing, the thatched grass crackling and sending showers of fiery sparks into the night air.

'Why?'

'I don't know. No . . . I remember now. Do they burn their wickiups when they're about to move camp?'

'You're the expert, Aunt Hilda,' I said. 'You're the famous explorer.'

'Hmm,' she said, moving uneasily with her bound hands. 'I might take up something a little more relaxing after this. Crochet?'

I couldn't help myself – the words just tumbled out. 'If there is an after.'

Aunt Hilda's neck craned and her eyes glowered. 'Never, ever, let me hear you speak like that again. I thought you weren't a quitter.'

'Sorry,' I mumbled, but my apologies were cut off by

a thunder of hooves and a great shouting as a party of horsemen rode into the camp. Braves rushed to help the new arrivals off the horses and the singers fell silent.

A very old man was at the centre of the party. He had a face as wrinkled as a walnut, topped with a thatch of white hair. He wore a decorated deerskin tunic and hat adorned with eagle feathers and porcupine quills. A quiver of arrows hung behind him. Riding beside him was a slim young woman, with a fall of black hair down her back and magnificent flashing eyes. She was dressed in a loose tunic and moccasins that came up to her thighs. A knife glinted from the right boot. The girl had a dashing, boyish air. Unlike the other Apaches, who were frightened to look at me, her eyes locked with mine. I saw she was curious and very excited.

The girl jumped off her horse and came striding towards me.

'I am Ish Kay Nay. In your language "Boy",' she said in English, with a Spanish accent.

I stared at her, bewildered. She had warlike stripes painted across her face in crimson and yellow. She was so bold in her movements and her voice was loud and confident. Not like the other Apache women, who had been timid and ran from me like startled deer.

'Why do they call you Boy?' I asked, because it seemed to me the most curious name in the world to call a girl.

'I am Apache girl and a warrior. I can shoot better and run faster – and some say I am cleverer – than a boy. So they call me Boy.'

'But you speak English?'

'I was captured by Mexicans. I learned Spanish and English. I told you, I learn quick – but no time now . . .' for behind her the old man was coming. His eyes were peering into mine, so deep-set in his walnut face that I was reminded of a tortoise peeping out of its shell.

Aunt Hilda was trying to stand up from her log, but was hobbled by her bound feet. She stood and then toppled over, dangerously close to the smoking fire. The girl grinned and helped her to her feet. All the while the old man was peering at me, gazing so hard I feared he would see into my soul.

I don't know why I was so afraid. I was not hiding anything. Or ashamed of who I was.

The old man grasped my hand and pulled me towards him. He was studying my arm and the snake branded on it. Then he dropped it, as if it burned him, and moved over to Cyril, sitting next to me. He gave his arm the same keen examination, then called the girl over to him.

'This is Nah Kay Yen,' she said. 'In your tongue "Far-Seeing Man".'

'Pleased to make your—' Aunt Hilda began, but the girl cut off her attempt at politeness.

'Far-Seeing Man is our medicine man, one of the greatest of the Apache nation,' the girl said. 'It is a great honour to you that he comes.'

She seemed to expect some answer, but none of us knew what to say. After an uncomfortable pause Boy glowered at us and her words came fast and furious.

'It is a time of big sadness. The White Eyes have brought death to the Apache. We are a small band, fighting for our lives against you Americans who herd us and starve us and kill us. You want to send us all to Fort Carlos to live like pigs on a reservation. We fight on. Yesterday we lost two warriors.'

A flash of understanding passed through me. The wailing, the mournful faces and burning huts. It had nothing to do with us, but was for the men they had lost in battle.

'For this we ought to punish, I tell Far-Seeing Man. We ought to punish all White Eyes. We ought to kill you all – but Apache are kinder than the stranger. We only charge the girl and the man—'

Far-Seeing Man barked at Boy and she stopped suddenly in the middle of her rant.

'The medicine man says it is not the time to speak of such things. He tells me he want to speak about *you*.'

At her words a stillness fell over us all. I had a glimpse of Waldo's terrified face and Rachel's big brown eyes as the girl continued.

'Far-Seeing Man knows all the trickery of witches. He can see the marks of magic and witchcraft through all the art that witches use. He speak the truth now.'

'This is nonsense,' Aunt Hilda blurted. But the medicine man spoke through her, his deep voice drowning hers. The girl listened and then interpreted.

'He has read the signs. He has looked and listened and consulted with the spirits. Usen has spoken. Please you and you get up.'

The girl pointed at Cyril Baker, then she turned her finger on me. Tottering a bit, we both stood. My legs were weak. I tried to calm myself to take whatever came now with the dignity of an Englishwoman. Behind me I heard Rachel moan and the low murmur of Waldo's voice.

'White Eyes: you, girl, Kit Salter. You, man, Cyril Baker. You stand before the creator, Usen, charged with unnatural acts, with using magic for evil.'

I wondered how Boy knew our names as she fell silent and turned to look at her shaman again. As far as I remembered, we had not told her. Far-Seeing Man was now chanting something, low sounds – soothing and lovely. A gentle melody before they hanged or scalped us. Boy was watching him. I saw something like wonder cross her face. She said something to him and he spoke sharply back.

Slowly the girl turned to us and spoke: 'Far-Seeing Man has decided. You are not witches.'

For a second the relief was so intense I thought I would collapse.

'What?' Baker gasped.

The girl shrugged. 'I do not understand his ways, but he *sees* so we must trust. He say you are no witch, so you are no witch.'

'We will not be scalped?' Cyril blurted out.

Boy's eyes flashed angrily. 'Apaches have never taken scalps. It is cruel. We do not know what this scalping is till you White Eyes bring it here.'

'Anyway,' I cut in hastily, 'are we free? Can we leave?'

Her wrath died down a little. 'Not so fast. Far-Seeing Man, he looks into your soul and sees bad things. He sees something very dark for you.' Her eyes moved slowly from Baker to me. 'On the ghost man and the girl there hangs a curse that, he says, glows stronger than the sun.'

'A curse,' I repeated slowly. *I* knew I was cursed, but how did the medicine man know?

'Someone is witching you. If he not drive the devil out – you will die.'

❧ Chapter Seventeen ❧

As the moon rose in the sky, the medicine man and Boy made preparations for our exorcism. Despite the protests of Aunt Hilda and Waldo, we were to take part in an Apache ceremony to drive the demons out of our souls.

Boy, who was the medicine man's assistant, was fascinated by me. She ordered us all to be freed from the ropes, and untied mine herself. They had left red weals on my ankles and wrists. As she worked, she asked questions. What were we doing on Apache land? When did the snake appear on our arms? Did we not know that snakes are bad, that the mark of a snake on us means great evil?

In turn I asked her questions, which she sometimes answered. When had she been taken captive? I asked. I learned, in bits and pieces, that she had been stolen along with her brother in a Mexican raid on an Apache village. She was just seven years old, her brother ten. The Mexicans and Apaches were old enemies. The Apaches raided the Mexicans' cattle and horses; the Mexicans tried to capture the Apaches as slaves.

135

When Boy was captured, her fate was slavery. She was put to work in a silver mine, digging all day long. She watched and learned – all sorts of things, like how to tell the time and speak English. One day her brother was shot for refusing to obey a petty order. The next day, seizing her chance, Boy escaped back to her tribe.

Though she didn't tell me this, I guessed that her bravery won admirers and that she grew to have a special status among the tribe. There had been an occasion when she narrowly avoided being struck by a bolt of lightning. Also, it must have been useful to them to have someone who knew the ways of the outside world, who could keep watch on their enemies, the Mexicans and the White Eyes or Americans.

Velvet night had fallen over the mountain by now. A mantle of stars and the nearly full moon hung low. The fire had been banked up and sent a wash of orange flaring over the camp. Boy had disappeared somewhere. I found myself alone with Waldo in the flickering firelight. Well, nearly alone. Rachel and the others were busy talking and not paying too much attention to us.

'I'm sorry,' he said to me, very low.

'For what?'

He didn't reply, letting the silence hang between us.

'What are you sorry for, Waldo?'

'You know.'

I gave him a sidelong glance. He looked so miserable I nearly relented. Steeling myself to be hard, I said,

'You tell me.'

'Why do you have to be such a beast, Kit?'

'*Me* . . . a beast?'

'You win. I've been horrible. Ghastly. Mean to you. There. Satisfied?'

'I just don't understand what I've done. I mean, why? I'd been in a coma for months. What could I have done wrong?'

He made a sound between a snort and a groan. 'You still don't know, do you?'

'No. I don't.'

'You've put me through so much – I didn't think I could stand –'

I didn't hear what he couldn't stand about me, because at that moment a chant began by the flickering fire. Masked men wearing swaying headdresses appeared, their bare chests daubed with paint. They began dancing around the flames, their legs pounding round and round in an increasing frenzy. While they danced, they sang. Not a song exactly, there were no words, but it was haunting nonetheless.

'Mountain spirits,' said Boy, who had reappeared by my side. 'The Gan dance.'

I think I recognised some of the boys who had been playing earlier, but I may have been mistaken because there was no way to make out features under the black masks. I realised that the rest of the tribe had gathered while I'd talked to Waldo. I had the sensation of pairs of eyes watching me, of murmured voices.

The shaman appeared at the head of three other medicine men, whose bodies were daubed with greenish blue. Each of the men had a yellow snake crawling up one arm to the shoulder. One had a yellow bear painted on his bare chest, another a flash of lightning. They wore kilts and moccasins and followed the shaman with bowed heads.

The shaman himself was splendid in a buckskin cloak and a medicine hat ornamented with eagle feathers and turquoise stones. From his seamed face, old eyes looked out, sought and enfolded me. When I looked at him, I felt as if I was falling into the deep sea.

The medicine man beat on a drum, leading the dancers, drawing us back to ancient times, the dawn of man's history: the wild flames raging over dark Apache eyes, the sweet smell of the juniper smoke, the ragged cries, the swaying figures with their eerie headdresses recalling monsters and devils, and around us the dark night, the coyotes, wolves, lynx and bear –the night hunters kept at bay by man's fires.

'Stand up!' Boy hissed in my ear, making me start.

I did as I was told, and she pushed Baker and me towards the medicine man. Baker stumbled, terrified. I caught him, feeling a surge of strength. My earlier wild imaginings had disappeared, dissolved in the strangeness all around us.

The medicine man began to mumble. His white hair gleamed in the moonlight as he puffed tobacco smoke out of a long pipe, which Boy wafted towards us. He was smoking strong-smelling herbs, which made me cough. But still Boy sent the smoke in our direction, scowling at our attempts to avoid it. When the shaman had smoked the whole pipe, Boy turned to us.

'Far-Seeing Man says that you are witched. Not by an Apache. By a Navajo medicine man. A skinwalker, a bad medicine man.'

I knew that the Navajos were another tribe of Indians who lived in these parts, but I didn't understand what Boy was talking about.

'These Navajo practise bad magic. Sometimes they are friend, sometimes our enemy.' Boy continued: 'The shaman, he say he has found bad medicine on you. You must find this thing and burn it.'

'Bad medicine? What does that mean?' Waldo asked.

'It means a curse. Someone has put a curse on your friend,' Boy said.

'It is common among these tribes to use fetishes, small objects with bad powers, to bring ill luck,' Aunt Hilda explained, but I wasn't listening to her. I knew we were cursed – the snake and the strange feeling in my head were proof of it. But I also understood the curse was older than these people – no Navajo medicine man was behind it.

'We must find the curse and pull it out,' Boy announced. 'This is important, Far-Seeing Man say, not just for you but for our tribe.'

Mr Baker and I looked at each other. We had been stripped clean; each of us now wore nothing but Apache clothes. From what Boy said, the curse was a thing, an object like a totem doll that could be burned. How could we have been cursed by an object when at this time we had not a thing to our names?

'We have nothing,' Mr Baker said. 'You took our clothes – and everything the robber left us.'

It took some time, but Boy sent a woman to fetch our clothes. She came scurrying back with an armful of stuff: Mr Baker's pale cream suit, my sensible travelling blouse and skirt and both our hats as well as two pairs of boots. Mr Baker's black boots, dusty now. My own stout brogues. Boy shook them out – there was clearly nothing there. No cursed object, no horrible twisted doll.

The shaman now came up to us slowly. He ignored the clothes, but picked up my left boot. It was of tan leather, with a small heel, pretty stitching and a rounded toe. A nice, comfortable brogue. Then he picked up Mr Baker's right boot, which looked to be of the softest, creamiest leather. He said something to Boy.

'The curse is here.' Boy indicated the boots the shaman held.

'No!' I shouted, because a rock had appeared in Boy's hand, like the one the women used to pound their flour. Now my brogue was in Boy's hand. She began to smash the heel of my shoe with the rock.

'I need that,' I said. 'I don't have any other shoes now.'

Too late. The bottom of the heel came off just before it split, revealing a small hollow. With a smile of triumph Boy picked something out of the heel. It was a fetish, gleaming white. No bigger than a bird's egg. She held it out to me and I took it with a trembling hand.

It was a tiny bird skull, spliced by a minute arrow ornamented with scraps of eagle feather. Running down the sides were scarlet threads, looking uncannily like tiny trickles of blood. Worst of all, gazing at the horrible thing I realised that a few hairs were glued to the skull.

My hairs.

Mr Baker had a similar object in his right boot. The look on his face, as he held it by the tips of his fingers, was sickening. He was terrified of this thing.

The medicine man was keening another of his wild songs as the totems were picked out of our unresisting hands and thrown into the fire.

'The curse must burn,' Boy said.

The tiny fetishes crackled for a few minutes and then

141

quickly burned down to ashes. Perhaps it was this wild setting, this camp of Apaches far from civilisation, that made me feel so strange. But as the fetishes crumbled to dust I felt a great burden lifting from me. My head no longer felt leaden, prickling with something else crawling around. No longer was I a listless body, driven on by some remaining spark of a person called Kit Salter.

We dismiss this Apache medicine as primitive, but I felt its power that night. I was at peace with the night. With bird, beast and the rest of the silent, waiting natural world. Whatever Far-Seeing Man had done to me was more effective than the powders and potions I had taken since I had come out of my coma. Much better than that mud bath I had so enjoyed.

I stood up and stretched. My heart sang with the new freedom. There was no longer a sick creature crawling in my head. My waking hours would no longer be filled with the sense of something trying to invade me, to fill my thoughts and take what it wanted.

KIT SALTER WAS BACK.

The shaman said something, looking at us, his filmy eyes full of sadness. Boy listened, then translated.

'The curse burns. You are free. You will stand tall. Tomorrow you can leave this place.'

❧ Chapter Eighteen ❧

As the shaman had decided that I was not a witch I was allowed to sleep in the wickiup with Aunt Hilda and Rachel. Boy announced she too would share our shelter, though I saw that she drew shocked glances from some of the other Apache women. She took no notice. I guessed that Boy usually got her own way.

'I am interested in you, Kit Salter,' she said, as we all curled up under the animal skins. The moon hung just above the firepit in the centre of the wickiup, its silver light streaming through the hole in the ceiling. 'You are an unusual White Eyes.'

'Thank you,' I said, 'if it's a compliment.'

Boy propped herself up on her elbow to look at me. She had the typical Apache smell, of grease and animal hides. Strong but not unpleasant when you got used to it.

'What is this? Compliment?'

'It means a good thing. If you're being kind about me.'

'It is neither kind nor unkind. It just is.' She turned to

143

Rachel. 'You, Rachel, are not different, I think. You will get married and have many children. Not Kit.'

'Kit will get married,' Rachel said. 'She'll probably get married before me.'

'No, I won't,' I said, blushing hotly.

'Don't want to be an old maid like me,' Aunt Hilda put in. 'Better snaffle up the first fellow that comes along.'

'Can you all stop talking about me and marriage? It's really embarrassing. I don't want to get married and—'

'What about Waldo?' Aunt Hilda interrupted. 'He's a pretty good catch. Better bag him before someone else comes along and takes his fancy.'

'Stop it!' I said. 'Would you all just leave me alone?'

Boy was sitting bolt upright, regarding us with amusement. Her eyes twinkled. 'Who is Waldo? Ah yes, the yellow-hair brave. Has he come to your wickiup with a horse?'

'What are you talking about?'

'In my people, when a boy wants to marry a girl he talks to her parents. If they agree, he takes a horse to her wickiup. If she feeds the horse, it means she consents. Has the yellow-hair brought his horse to you?'

'It doesn't happen like that among us,' I said stiffly, while Aunt Hilda and Rachel guffawed. But Boy's eyes were on me, unsmiling. She was deadly serious.

'I look at you, Kit, and I do not think this is your

path. You are a warrior, like me. This is why I am your friend.'

'You must be quite unusual among the Apaches.'

She shrugged her shoulders. 'I fight. By fighting and by wisdom I get much honour. But it has been hard. When my brother was killed, I knew this was the path I must take. You too, I think, have a hard road. You have the signs of being set apart. I can see great struggle for you and maybe great wisdom. Marriage is not—'

'I feel very sleepy,' I said, interrupting her, because I could guess what she was saying. She seemed convinced that a normal life of marriage wasn't for me. Maybe she was right, but I was far too young to think about such things. Why did everyone talk such nonsense? Anyway, what did this wild girl know about me? 'Do you think we could all go to sleep, please?'

So we settled down for the night. I think the others were soon fast asleep, but I stayed awake thinking over the events of the past days. The shaman with his mystical powers. The chilling fetishes in our shoes. Who had put them there?

Well, that at least I could answer. Cecil Baker. But what purpose the ugly little fetishes served I did not know. Witchcraft, the shaman had said. What would a man born in nineteenth-century England, brought up in the modern world, know about witchcraft? The whole thing was absurd, with its aura of Stone Age magic, a belief in demons and spirits that had surely vanished with the coming of the railways, the flushing WC and gas lighting.

Thinking such thoughts, I drifted off to sleep with the muffled hush of the night camp in my ears. Aunt Hilda's snoring, Boy's soft breathing. Behind it all the murmur of the wind through the pinyon pines and the shush of prowling night creatures. It was very peaceful and I felt safe. Which was strange when you consider I was still a prisoner of the Apaches. Somehow I knew that Boy would never harm me, if only because she seemed convinced that I was her White Eyes twin!

I woke with a jerk. My dreams had been full of dancers swaying above me with the faces of dogs and pigs. I think I'd been asleep several hours as my limbs felt stiff and my mouth tasted sour. By the weak moonlight I could see the others were still sleeping.

Something was snuffling at the door, trying to get in past the deerskin that covered it.

I rose quietly, thinking it was most likely some small animal I could shoo away. I put on the long moccasins that Boy had given me in place of my boots. I was just removing the hide from the hole in the wickiup that served as a door when Boy awoke, bleary-eyed.

'What are you doing?'

'There's something out there. I'm just going to check that an animal isn't hurt.'

'NO, KIT. COME BACK HERE!'

Too late. I was already out of the wickiup. I closed the flap of skin and looked around me. The mountain wind was high, and it was chilly without the blazing fire to keep us warm. A wash of rainclouds hung low over the mountains, which I knew would please the Apaches, who longed for the rains.

The moon bathed the camp in enough light to see it was quiet. I saw no humans moving around, or animals. Just the hairy domes of the Apache homes, with their inhabitants asleep inside. But I had definitely heard something. Snuffling breath around the wickiups, with something hard scratching the earth.

I bent down and could see the faint tracks of some creature. Why had it been so determined to get into our tent? I decided to follow it and moved towards the outskirts of the camp. I heard Boy moving behind me, calling softly out to me from the wickiup.

'Where are you going? Come back. Come back.'

There were several large thorny bushes dotted around the edge of the camp, shading into the ever-present pinyon pines. Walking towards them, I noticed a movement in the shadows and heard the snapping of twigs.

Calling softly, I moved towards the bush. In a flash, a dark shape jumped out of the bush and dashed away. It seemed strangely furtive, keeping out of the patches of moonlight, lurking in the shadows. It was a big animal, and for a moment I was scared and thought I would go back to the wickiup. But on second thoughts it was moving so clumsily I was sure it was injured.

An injured horse – or deer. By its running shape I could tell it was on four legs and so not a bear.

Still calling, I moved stealthily towards the other clump of bushes in which it had taken shelter. Poor thing, it was so clumsy.

I gained on the bushes and then suddenly the thing charged out, running straight for me. At the last minute it veered off in another direction into another bush. At the edge of it, it turned its head with a jerky movement, and stopped and looked at me.

I am an English girl. I have been brought up in Oxford, taught by a succession of governesses. Though I have travelled a lot, I am not used to life in the wilds. But even I knew something was seriously wrong with this deer. It did not run as a normal four-legged creature would, its gait elegant and loping. The movement of one living thing is different from another; even the city dweller would not mistake a running horse for a running deer, or a flying duck for a swallow.

But this deer ran in a very odd manner, halfway, indeed, between a horse and a human. In the bright patch of moonlight I could see it held its head up straight, its neck stretched right out. A huge pair of antlers quivered above its head. Its eyes stared at me, the pupils flaring in yellowish pools. Strange to say, the eyes were dull. This will sound fanciful, but it was looking at me with malice.

The deer hated me, Kit Salter.

Boy was breathing hard behind me.

'What an odd deer,' I said.

'That's no deer.'

'Look at its antlers.'

Roughly, from behind, Boy pushed me aside. 'Stand back.'

As I turned, she raised her shotgun and fired. The bullet whizzed past me, smacking bang into the flank of the deer.

'NO!' I screamed.

Boy shot again. And again. The bangs reverberating through the camp.

'Stop it!' I shouted. I ran towards the deer as fast as I could, Boy yelling at me. Fury coursed through me. That animal had done nothing to Boy and she had callously shot it. The deer looked at me, one last long glare through eyes that did not shine, then bounded clumsily off.

I saw it being shot. I saw at least two bullets burying themselves in its flank. Yet it had sped off, as if nothing had happened.

All around, people were emerging from their wickiups,

roused by the bangs. I had a glimpse of Waldo, and Mr Baker, who had fallen down on the ground and was rolling over and over. Then I fell down as well, the world turning black.

⚬⚬⚬⚬

When I woke up, the first thing I saw was the ground swishing under me from side to side. I was skimming over it, like a gliding bird. I looked up and saw a pink cheek and a lock of blond hair.

'Put me down, Waldo.'

'No need to shout about it.'

He hoisted me off his shoulders and plonked me down. I got to my feet, a little unsteadily. All the others were crowding round me, Aunt Hilda, Rachel. I saw Isaac was carrying Cyril Baker slung over his shoulders.

'What's wrong with him?'

Isaac shrugged. 'He fainted.'

'Always thought he was a bit potty,' Aunt Hilda said.

'He fainted at the same instant as you,' Rachel said.

My eye fell on Boy, who was standing next to Aunt Hilda, her eyes flashing from her copper face.

'Why did you shoot? That deer meant us no harm.'

'It was no deer. I have already told you this.'

I stared at her, absolutely bewildered. 'Of course it was a deer. You saw its antlers.'

150

'That was not a deer it was a . . .' and Boy said a word in her language I didn't understand.

'A what?'

'A skinwalker.'

'A skinwalker?' I had no idea of what she meant, though I had a vague memory of hearing the word before.

'A skinwalker is a bad medicine man. One who can transform into the shape of any animal. No one knows who the skinwalker is. By day they pretend to be a kind, right-living person. A medicine man who helps all.

'Then by night they transform into an animal and they go through the country doing evil. As soon as I saw the tracks I knew that was no deer. I knew it was a skinwalker. Now I have proof.'

'How?'

'You cannot kill a skinwalker. I put three bullets in its body and not a single drop of blood. This is proof.

'This skinwalker wishes you harm, Kit. If you had let it in the wickiup, evil would have befallen us all. The skinwalker was entering your mind. When you came near, it had its chance. You and that man –' she waved at the waxy-faced Baker – 'the thing that made you both fall down was the skinwalker leaving your soul. The shock of separation made you – how do you say? – made you a little bit crazy.'

None of this made much sense to me. But something she'd said before struck me.

151

'What about the tracks?' I asked. 'I can't understand how you can tell by an animal's tracks that it is a skinwalker.'

Boy glanced at me, superiority in her big black eyes. Her plump mouth was curling upwards, as if she found my ignorance comical but charming. 'Come with me.'

She led the way back to the wickiup. Waldo, Rachel and Aunt Hilda followed, while Isaac and a crowd of awakened Apaches stayed with the still unconscious Baker. There Boy squatted and showed me the deer prints. I am no tracker, but I could see that they were strange indeed. Rather than following each other as a dog's or horse's will do, these deer tracks were at all sorts of odd angles. They were also spread apart, as if the deer had been walking with its legs right open. Walking like a man would do.

That was it. If anything, the tracks looked like they'd been made by a man walking, wearing deer-hoof shoes.

'The skinwalker's footprints,' said Boy.

❧ Chapter Nineteen ❧

When I woke up the next morning, the eerie happenings of the night before seemed a bad dream. No trace remained of the chase through the bushes except a few broken twigs. Had that nocturnal ramble been a fairytale? Some witchery that had sneaked into my mind? With the sun blazing hot above us, normality had returned.

We had a sombre breakfast around the still-smoking juniper-wood fire. We ate hash made from mescal, the paste I had seen the women grinding, with the juicy flesh of a cactus and ripe berries. I enjoyed the unusual meal, overhung as it was with the scent of smoke and earth. Somehow food always tastes better out in the wild.

Food, though, was the last thing on any of our minds. Cyril Baker had not recovered from his faint. I went to see him in the wickiup he shared with Waldo and Isaac, where he lay under a pile of animal skins. He looked pale. Of course he always looked pale; even at the best of times the man was a living ghost. But now there was a bluish tinge to his pallor. It was ghastly to look at him, and to my shame

I felt a desperate need to get away. I restrained myself and put a hand on the white arm that rested on the skins.

'Cyril,' I said. His arm was cold and damp. 'Can you hear me?'

He did not stir.

'Cyril, it's me, Kit Salter. Can I do anything to help?'

There was not a flicker in his gingery lashes, not a tremble to show he had heard my voice. Waldo was beside me. He coughed and I glanced at his face. His expression was strained, almost as ghastly as Cyril's.

'What *is* the matter, Waldo?' I asked.

'I can't stand it any longer,' he muttered, and crashed out of the tent.

I stayed a little longer, talking to Mr Baker, speaking kindly to him; I felt more affection for the man than ever before. I was just telling him I believed he was good, would have lived a better life if it wasn't for his brother's evil influence, when he opened his eyes and smiled at me.

'I'm glad you still think there's hope for my soul,' he said. 'It's a great comfort.'

I reddened, for I had been babbling on in the belief he was unconscious.

'You do understand, Kit, what happened last night?'

I nodded. I felt it, his brother's dark presence.

'Cecil visited this camp.'

'The deer?' I asked. 'He controlled the deer?'

'Yes, the deer *was* Cecil. It must be one of the many shapes he can take at will. He has become a more powerful skinwalker than I ever imagined, Kit. Before I left his side, he would strain to leave his body for an instant. It would be a great task to flit into the body of a pigeon for the merest moments. Now he attacks us openly in the guise of a deer.'

'It was only a deer, not something ferocious,' I said. 'I mean, couldn't he have been a bear if he'd wanted to attack us?'

Cyril waved his arms. 'You miss the point. It was a warning. Cecil was warning us all, especially me. He was showing me his power.'

'Boy has explained about skinwalking,' I said, slowly, 'but I don't really understand. What is your brother's game?'

'As I've told you, he studied the native Indian arts and the black arts for many years. He has great mystical power. You know he is sick, Kit. He is dying. He believes he can cheat death by leaving his body and taking on other forms. This is why he studied the ancient Indian magic for so long.'

'So – it's like a trick he's playing on his own destiny? His body is infected with the Himalayan curse, so he leaves it and takes possession of another creature?'

'Yes, but there are limits to his power. I believe he can only invade another skin for a short time.'

I looked at him for a long moment, the silence heavy between us. Everything seemed to have gone dark, and I was haunted by fears I couldn't easily name. Cyril Baker didn't help; he just gazed at me with those strangely empty eyes.

'This is awful,' I said finally. 'It means your brother could be anywhere . . . spying on us, trapping us.' I indicated the world through the flap of the wickiup, a peaceful scene of hairy tents and Indians in the sunshine. 'Cecil could be in that humming-bird hovering over the cacti, or the eagle that swoops over us while we ride in the desert. In the raccoon or the skunk under our horses' hoofs—'

'Enough!' Cyril raised his hand. 'Don't let fear infect you, else Cecil has won.'

⣎⣿⣒

When I emerged from the wickiup, the camp was in the midst of preparations for our departure. Even the ancient medicine man had emerged from his tent to see us on our way. He had selected, personally, a horse for me to ride. He indicated which one it was, his dark eyes shining under his thatch of white hair. The horse was a magnificent stallion called Rolling Thunder. Apparently it was a great honour for me, that the famous Far-Seeing Man had himself selected my horse. It showed he liked us and wished us well.

The Apaches were generous to give us several horses, as they were clearly poor and in the midst of a dangerous war with two enemies: the American settlers they called

156

White Eyes and the Mexicans. I did not think these brave warriors had much chance of survival. Even if the Apaches had stolen and mastered the art of shooting with guns, the Americans would counter with more powerful weapons. What use was an ancient musket against a howitzer or a cannon?

These thoughts were running through my head as we mounted our horses. We were provisioned with some of their mescal paste, a few strips of dried meat and fresh water in our canisters. The Apaches had returned our own clothes, freshly washed and dried in the sun. But Mr Baker and I both wore deerskin moccasins. Embroidered with beautiful patterns, they came up to my knees and were very soft. Sadly, Baker could not ride and had been propped up behind Waldo on a roan stallion. Waldo was chosen as he was the best rider.

As Waldo took directions to the nearest town, a day and more of hard riding away, I said a silent goodbye to the Apache camp with its wickiups lit up by the streaky sunshine filtering through the pinyon pines, the brook burbling in the distance, the horses chewing contentedly. And the people: the women in their bright beads and buckskins, busy at their domestic tasks; the infants scrabbling besides their mothers; the children playing with bows and arrows. It looked a peaceful, time-honoured scene. Then Boy was at my shoulder, her round face showing sadness.

'I come with you,' she said. 'I like you, so I will be your guide.'

'You hardly know me.'

'It doesn't matter. I spend much time with Far-Seeing Man. Now I too can see into people souls. You and me, we are –' Boy stopped short, blinking hard and looking into the distance. 'Maybe it is not safe for you alone. There are Apaches in the mountains.'

'But, Boy, *you* are an Apache.'

'Other Apaches. Hostiles.'

'Would you really want that? To go back to the world of white settlers? To civilisation?'

She shuddered, biting her lip. 'I never want be civilised again.'

I had to laugh at that – she said it with such ferocity. Silly to say, but her sudden fierce attachment had produced an answering affection in me. She was so hot-headed, with her eyes flashing with indignation. It must have been hard for her to be accepted as a warrior in a world where women on the whole were wives and mothers, content with domestic work. Boy was a funny thing – odd name and all.

But had I been silly to dismiss her? She had shown real bravery last night, fighting the skinwalker. I was going to shake Boy's hand, because I could hardly embrace her, but she moved away. I understood then that she did not want me to touch her. For a moment I was offended, then

I realised it must seem a strange custom to these Apaches to shake hands.

'I will fight the civilised forever,' she said, holding her hands behind her back. 'The White Eyes are cruel and have no respect for the earth or the sky.'

The shaman had appeared at her side and said something to her. She listened, replied angrily and then turned to me. 'Far-Seeing Man, he says the White Eyes' day is coming. He says the White Eyes will rule all . . . He speaks truly, always, but this I can't believe.'

I looked from Boy to Far-Seeing Man and a wave of sadness overwhelmed me. The shaman indeed must be wise to see this future. It struck me as already happening. Many groups of Indians had been defeated by the American settlers, rounded up and sent to live on reservations. Others had been felled in their hundreds of thousands by the diseases that the white man brought with him in his huge ships. Smallpox was fatal, but even relatively mild illnesses like chickenpox and measles killed countless Indians.

Looking at the wickiups and the smoke drifting in the sunshine, I could see no future for this way of life. It was vanishing, and would soon be just a part of history. Better that the Apaches surrendered than be brutally cut down amidst more bloodshed.

'He speaks the truth,' I said. 'Nothing, I think, can stop the White Eyes.'

Far-Seeing Man held up a hand, almost as if he understood my words, and spoke rapidly to Boy, who listened with her head tilted.

'The White Eyes' day is coming, but Far-Seeing Man says his day will also end,' she translated. 'The foreigners, they do not love the earth that gives us life, but scar it with great gashes of rock and rivers of iron. They dig up its soul looking for silver and gold. The earth is not mother and father to them, but only something they can own. So they will destroy it and in the end the earth will rise up—'

Her words were interrupted because Far-Man began to talk. His eyes rolled so all I could see were the whites. The pupils had almost vanished. A high thin voice came out of his mouth, a voice that spoke English:

'The Black Snake is coming. To the land of the White Sun.'

❧ Chapter Twenty ❧

We had no maps to guide us to the small mining camp, which Boy had said was home to the nearest white men. I rode Rolling Thunder savagely, with desperate speed, through the twisting mountain paths, downwards to the arid desert. As we rode, we prayed we were going in the right direction. Several times I wished I had taken up Boy's offer to be our eyes and ears. Having someone who knew exactly which way to go might make the difference in saving Cyril's life.

He was desperately ill. He had come back to consciousness in a state of high fever. He spoke in wild, disconnected sentences about snakes and his beloved twin. His face was white, white as a dying moon. Yellow pus collected in his eyes and dribbled down his face. The last thing he needed was to be ridden so hard, propped up like a tailor's dummy behind Waldo.

❧❧❧

We stopped for lunch after four or five hours' riding. Cyril's hands were burning hot. I helped Waldo bring him down

161

from the horse. We propped him against a pinyon pine and poured a little water into his mouth. His eyes were rolling around as if seeking something. Perhaps he was looking for his brother. When Waldo went to help prepare our basic meal, I tried to get him to eat some dried deer meat, but he shook his head in refusal. Then he groaned, because the motion was painful.

'Be still,' I said. 'Don't move if it hurts.'

'I'm sorry, Tabby,' Mr Baker replied in a clear voice, looking straight in my eyes. 'We never meant you any harm, Tabby.'

I froze. Tabby. It was the affectionate family nickname for my mother, my long-dead mother. Her name was Tabitha, but my father always used to refer to her as Tabby. I had a fuzzy memory of calling her that myself.

My mother, Tabitha . . . Tabby.

But how could Mr Baker know?

I must have misheard. Or had I used the name when my mother's oval locket was stolen by the bandit?

It was several minutes before I could compose myself to ask the question.

'Are you speaking of my mother, Tabitha – Tabby?' I asked. 'How do you know her nickname?'

But that flash of lucidity in his eyes had gone. They now swung dully over me – and to the barren lands beyond.

I ate the rest of my dried meat and berries. Tabby? He had repeated it, said it twice. Did it have some other meaning? Or was Mr Baker apologising for some harm he had done my mother? The very idea was ridiculous. She had died long before he had come into our lives.

As we rode on after our brief rest, questions tormented me. Everything conspired to make me uneasy. The snake on my arm, wriggling each day. The skinwalker. The shaman's odd words about a snake and a white sun – which set off strange echoes in my mind. Now this. Mr Baker's mention of my mother. None of it made any sense.

Mr Baker himself was in a desperate state, but all of us were very weary by the time we rode over the brow of the mountain and sighted the mining camp. From the distance it was a ramshackle affair, a few clapboard houses in the middle of a series of rocky heaps where precious metals had been dug from the earth. What a relief the sight was. It had been hard riding through the day and much of the night. My legs and thighs ached; my vision was blurred by dust and sand.

The sun was setting over the mountains when we rode into the camp. Grimy miners were returning from their day's work. The place had a bit more to it than I had first thought. A saloon bar, a hotel of sorts, a grocery store and a jail, off the beaten dust track. We rode down the main street and every eye in the place

163

turned on us. I felt a swell of pride at riding behind Waldo. In his cowboy hat, his blue eyes gleaming, he was a fine leader.

'Howdy,' he called out. 'We got a sick man here. Is there a doctor in town?'

A huddle of men in those rough blue overalls, carrying pickaxes and shovels, turned their eyes on Waldo and the limp figure of Cyril Baker behind him. It needed but a single glance to see that Baker was dying. But nobody said a word; all eyes just rested on us.

One man who was chewing a wad of tobacco spat it in our direction. It landed on the ground in front of my stallion, just missing the horse. There were a few chuckles at that.

'Please help. We're peaceful folk, American patriots,' Waldo said. 'We need your help.'

I would have done anything for Waldo after an appeal like that, but in this hostile hick town nobody moved. From the direction of the saloon next to us I heard twanging guitars and a gust of wild laughter.

'For goodness' sake,' Aunt Hilda burst out. 'Are you all numbskulls? We need a doctor fast!'

At that there were a few resentful murmurs. The man who had spat tobacco in our direction turned to a dull-looking man with a bull neck standing beside him and said, 'Better call Dobie.'

'Dobie?' Bull Neck asked, his mind moving with the slowness of a beetle.

'Yeah, Red Dobie,' the first man replied.

I looked at the bunch of miners despairingly. They were tough, weather-beaten men, their skin tanned by the harsh sun and scoured by the sand and grime of the mines. They had wrinkled faces and a stunted look of surly hostility. I had heard these parts were primitive and savage; the white settlers as well as the Indians were said to resent outsiders. Life was of less value out here, in this Wild West, than gold or bullets.

But these men seemed to be positive halfwits. We had done them no harm, Cyril Baker was clearly dying and yet they stood there gazing at us like a herd of cattle.

At that moment the door to the Last-Dance Saloon swung open and a tall man strode out. He wore a wide-brimmed cowboy hat, and a couple of holsters on his belt each contained a pistol. He strode towards us, his spurs jangling.

'Who might you be?' he drawled.

All at once a prattle of voices rose up. 'Dobie. Red. Strangers. Got Carlito. What you gonna do, Red?'

Dobie Red, if that was his name, held up his hand and the voices stopped. A star-shaped badge glinted on his waistcoat, inscribed with the legend SHERIFF.

Slowly he took a puff on his cigarette, then blew the smoke out towards Waldo.

'You ain't answered my question. Coyote got your tongue? I asked you what yer doin' in my town.'

'It's a long story,' Waldo replied. 'The short version is that we come in peace. We got a sick man here and we need to find a doctor.'

Dobie Red – or Red Dobie – glanced at Cyril, slumped behind Waldo on his horse. It took but a second to see that he was desperately ill, his breath rattling out of his chest.

'Looks pretty bad,' Red agreed.

'Have you a doctor here?'

'Yeah. We got a doctor.'

'Well, we've no time to waste. We need to get this man there. Please.'

Red held up a hand. When he lowered it, we saw a Colt glinting in his grip. 'Not so fast. I'm gonna have to arrest you first.'

The pistol was pointing straight at me.

I exhaled slowly. Meanwhile Aunt Hilda had started to splutter. I stared at the sheriff, bewildered. Wasn't that the name for a policeman out in these parts? Why was it that everyone in America seemed to pull a gun on us?

'What is it I'm supposed to have done?' I asked.

'No supposin' about it. I know you're a lady, but that ain't ladylike behaviour now, is it?'

'Why are you arresting me? You've only just met me.'

'Got the evidence right here. Take you to Redwood City for trial. If you weren't a lady, expect you'd get the maximum penalty.'

'For what? What am I supposed to have done?'

The menace in the man's voice made us all fearful. Aunt Hilda urged her horse on. It trotted up so that it stood by my side.

'For heaven's sake, man,' she said, in her most imperious voice. 'Tell us straight out. Why are you accusing my niece? I'm certain it will all turn out to be a ghastly mistake.'

Even out here in the wilds of the West I could see that Aunt Hilda's tone commanded respect. The sheriff gazed up at her, his gun never wavering from my throat.

'No disrespect, ma'am, but your niece here, she done a bad thing.'

'Explain yourself, man.'

'She's a horse thief.' Red waved his gun at my magnificent stallion, the one the shaman had given me personally, the one called Rolling Thunder. 'That li'l beaut she's riding is my own Carlito.'

The crowd started to mutter. 'That's right, it's Carlito . . . Damn rustlers . . . Knew it at once, never mistook a horse in my life . . .'

Trust me to ride into a mining camp full of toughs on one of their own stolen horses. This would take some explaining. The mob was getting angrier, mutters turning into fingered guns. How long before their words turned to action, to sticks and stones? Red sensed this because he raised his gun and fired a warning shot into the air. It startled my Rolling Thunder. He reared up, but I managed to get him under control.

'Quieten down,' Red shouted. 'Carlito is my horse and I'm gonna do this my way. The civilised law-abiding way. We ain't having no lynching here.'

'What's lynching?' Rachel whispered, as the crowd shuffled at Red's words. It was too awful to explain to her. Lynching meant a mob acting without rule of law, beating someone they took a dislike to, hanging them from a tree or a post. Hanging them till they were stone dead.

'We gonna ride this young lady to the jail. We gonna see proper justice even if it means taking her all the way to Tombstone or Yuma. But I'm gonna do this by the law, you hear?' Red drawled – and my heart lightened a bit. 'We do it proper – and *then* you git to see one or two of these here rogues hanged.'

With the gun in my face and the angry mob surrounding me, I could not think of a single thing to say. Aunt Hilda was made of sterner stuff.

'Do you know who I am?' she demanded of the sheriff.

'No, ma'am.'

'I'm Lady Hilda Salter, world-famous explorer and

second cousin of Queen Victoria of England. This is the honourable Katherine Salter, daughter of the Duke of Devonshire. She will be a duchess one day.'

'Don't make no difference to me. We are freeborn American citizens – we don't owe your queen nothing.'

His words were defiant, but I noticed that one or two of the men had started shuffling uneasily.

'I've travelled through the wilds of the Himalayas and the darkest jungles of Africa. I've received more courtesy from the Sultan of Borneo – a notoriously bloodthirsty man – than I have from you so-called civilised Americans. Will you hear our story?'

'Better listen, Red,' a sandy-haired youth called out, and other voices rose in agreement. Red nodded and Aunt Hilda began her tale. Truthfully she told how we left San Francisco and journeyed to Calistoga where we picked up a stagecoach and came out to Arizona. Equally truthfully she related how we had been held up by a lone outlaw, who had stripped us of everything we owned.

At the description of the trick that had been played on us, the single outlaw who had made us believe he commanded a gang of robbers, many of the miners broke out into guffaws. He was notorious in these parts, apparently, and went by the name of Bandit Bart.

It was quite a distinction to have been robbed by him – these miners gazed on us with new respect.

Then Waldo interrupted and took up the story of how we had been kidnapped by Apaches. Aunt Hilda was quite annoyed that he had butted in, but I could see he had some plan. I was tense as I listened, for I didn't want to betray our Apache friends. In the end they had treated us quite decently. Even though they had clearly stolen Red Dobie's magnificent horse, well, they had sort of given it back, hadn't they? I did not want to betray their trust.

Waldo did not let me down. He didn't tell the miners how the Apaches had let us go, giving us food, water and horses. Instead he related how we had escaped in the dead of night, stealing their horses and riding through night and day to this place. The Apaches were the thieves, he declared, not us. Cyril Baker was dying because the Indians had beaten him so savagely.

His story, I could see, had turned the tables.

But still Red Dobie was suspicious. He turned to me, his eyes blazing. 'What about those?' he asked, pointing to the embroidered moccasin boots I wore. 'How come you all dressed up like a fancy Indian squaw?'

My heart fluttered and for a moment I couldn't speak. 'The Apaches stole my boots,' I said. 'Seemed only fair that I *borrow* a pair of theirs.'

A huge laugh rose from the crowd at my words. Several of those rugged, sunburnt miners were rolling around as if I had said the wittiest thing ever. It was *that* funny.

170

'We've been through hell and come out the other side,' Aunt Hilda broke in. 'Now will you let us take this man to the doctor?'

Red signalled with his gun and a couple of young men came over to Waldo, with Mr Baker lying limp behind him. 'Take him to Doc Cotton's,' he said. 'Make sure he gets the best treatment.' He spread his legs wide and grinned up to him. 'Say Red Dobie's gonna foot the bill – after all, these strangers brought my Carlito back home.'

'Thank you,' Aunt Hilda said. 'That's . . . well, mighty gracious of you.'

Red waved his pistol in the air as if to say it was nothing. Then, to my relief, he put it back in his holster. 'In return I need your help for something. Can you tell me where those Apaches are hiding out? I'm gonna get a party of men to—'

'Flush 'em out,' Waldo interrupted.

'Yeah. We need to do a little spring cleaning out here.'

I was seized with anguish; if we were to bring death to the Apaches as the price of saving our skins, I would never forgive myself. I had a sudden vivid flash of the Apache camp. The settlers riding through it on horseback, setting fire to the wickiups, shooting women and children, whoever happened to be around. And if the warriors were there, including my own brave friend Boy, that would be worse.

A massacre.

'The Apache camp is over there,' Waldo said, indicating the direction we had come from. 'I'll tell you exactly how to find it.'

To my horror he gave a detailed description of the camp – and the Indians who lived there – right down to the eagle-shaped stone guarding the entrance. Bile rose from my stomach into my mouth and for an instant I could hardly breathe. The sun shining on his blond hair, his blue eyes glowing, Waldo calmly betrayed every detail. A shimmering veil of anger covered my eyes as I gazed at him and heard the words coming out of his mouth. So he had meant those things he'd said about the Apaches; he thought they were savages who deserved to be enslaved or put to death.

It didn't matter how handsome and amusing Waldo was, I could never, ever feel friendship for him again.

Rachel was as shocked as I was. She looked at him, her eyes widening, the colour draining from her face. As we moved towards Doc Cotton's surgery, a posse of cowboys gathered. They raised a cloud of dust as they galloped over the desert towards the distant mountains.

A cloud of dust that signalled death to the Apache camp.

❧ Chapter Twenty-one ❧

Past Bill Sherman's General Store was a sign swinging on an iron hook saying COTTON'S SURGERY. It was illustrated with a picture of a cowboy with his arms round a grizzly bear. The man I took to be the doc was sitting on the porch, swinging back and forth on a rocking chair while he puffed on a pipe. A grubby child played with a hoop and stick beside him. When he saw a crowd of people rushing towards him, carrying a body on a stretcher, the doc jumped up, knocking his pipe out.

'Trouble?'

'No shooting today,' one of the stretcher bearers replied. 'This man's real sick.'

'Bring him in.'

The five of us went in with the stretcher bearers – who laid Cyril out on the bare pine table. It was clean enough, but I saw deep scratches on it and ragged dark stains. Perhaps of blood. Cyril was bad; he was spectral, burning up. His eyes were open, but looked at nothing.

I was frightened for him.

Doc Cotton ripped open his shirt. A bony lad, apparently his assistant, had appeared. He brought a pail of water, with which the doctor sluiced down Cyril's chest.

'He's mighty hot,' he said. 'Got any idea how he catched this fever?'

Aunt Hilda shrugged. 'Not really. He seemed a little poorly in California – just got worse and worse as we came into the desert.'

'Poor wretch shouldn't have travelled. What's the hurry anyway?'

'He believed he was cursed,' I said.

Doc Cotton swung his gaze over to me, his pale blue eyes widening. 'Cursed?'

'Something like that,' I said, aware of how foolish I sounded. 'He believed he was struck down with an illness that wasn't of – I don't know – of human origin . . . Like a disease of the spirit . . . that he was haunted, if you—'

'The child is confused,' Aunt Hilda butted in. 'She doesn't know what she's saying. Mr Baker here caught a fever – that is all.'

'Sounds like Apache talk,' said Doc Cotton, keeping his eyes trained on me. 'Or them Navajo Indians. They talk of ghost sickness. That's when the dead come back to haunt the living.'

'Maybe it involves a skinwalker,' I said.

174

'That one of them savages who can turn themselves into animals?'

'I think the idea is that they can walk – literally walk – in other creatures' skins.'

'You can't believe in such nonsense,' Aunt Hilda interrupted, but Doc Cotton just shrugged.

While we were talking, the gangling assistant had been removing Baker's shirt and trousers. He was near naked now, his skinny body laid out on the slab as if being prepared for his funeral, so pale it could have been made out of glue, or dried cheese. The brand of the snake was very visible on him – but now it was no longer on his arm. It had appeared instead in the centre of his chest, just to the right of his heart.

'What's that?' the doctor asked, staring at it.

'Witchery,' I replied, while Aunt Hilda hurriedly said it was some sort of decoration.

'Skinwalkers and suchlike,' the doctor said, 'I don't know much about 'em. But I don't hold with dismissing it out of hand. The desert ain't like the city.'

'Men turning into animals?' Waldo asked in a sceptical voice. 'Sounds like heathen poppycock.'

I glared at him when he spoke, then glanced away. At the moment, feeling as I did, I never wanted to see his smug face ever again.

'Stranger things have happened out here.'

The doctor began to palpate the chest, placing his hands firmly over Cyril's body. He grunted something to his assistant who went over to the wall and fetched a pair of large rusty-looking pliers and a pair of tongs. I thought it strange that the doctor didn't order us out of the surgery while he was working. No other doctor I've known would operate on someone with an audience crowding around. Waldo, Isaac and Aunt Hilda were gazing with a sort of ghoulish curiosity as the doctor swabbed down Cyril's chest, but Rachel was looking rather sick.

'I think he got some kind of stone or blockage down here,' the doctor said. 'Feels hard. Like summin's wrong. First I'm gonna take some of his blood. 'After doing some tests I'm gonna make a li'l cut just here' – he pointed to the snake on Cyril's chest – 'and take a closer look inside.'

It was my friend down there on the table, helpless as a goat about to be skinned. My initial suspicion and dislike of him had vanished. Our illness, too, had made a bond between us. Still, I wondered how well I really knew him. Often his presence felt as slippery as satin. Something that would slide through your fingers, leaving you unsure of what you were dealing with.

We were in the same boat, Cyril Baker and I. It was just that he was further down the road. I hadn't wanted to explain to the doctor the origin of our illness. How we were both cursed by drinking an elixir of life, a forbidden

176

water in the Himalayas. How a worm of disease, a grub of illness, had feasted on us ever since. Growing fat on our souls. How could I explain something like that to a simple country doctor?

It was easier to put it in Apache terms. I turned away from the scene around the operating table and gazed around aimlessly. Mr Baker was haunted by ghost sickness. Something was not right inside him; he had a diseased soul.

While I was thinking these thoughts, my eyes were idly swinging over Doc Cotton's cabinets. The trophy cabinet was stuffed with moose head, deer antler and buffalo skins. The diagram of a horse, with all the major bones and arteries. The skull of a dog, or was it a sheep?

An awful lot of pictures of animals. He must love animals.

'Most of your patients aren't much given to conversation, are they, Doc Cotton?' Isaac said loudly, cutting into my thoughts. I turned round just as the doctor filled a syringe with Baker's blood.

'They're not exactly fine talkers,' he replied.

I stared at him, strange suspicions forming in my mind.

'What are you blathering about, Isaac?' Aunt Hilda said, her eyes glued on the syringe. 'Stop interrupting. The doctor's got work to do.'

'The veterinarian,' Isaac said.

'What?'

'Doc Cotton's main business is animals, not humans. Isn't that right, Doc?' Isaac said.

'People can't afford to be too choosy around here,' the man replied. 'There ain't another medical man within a hundred miles . . . So I do get more than my fair share of humans.'

'Gunshot wounds mostly, I'd guess,' Isaac said, looking at the pliers.

'Nobody better at taking lead from a man's gut than Doc Cotton,' the skinny assistant piped up loyally.

'You're a veterinarian?' I asked, appalled.

'By training, yep. But jack of all trades out here.'

Aunt Hilda had flushed deep red. 'Sir . . . you have played the foulest trick on us.'

Sighing, Doc Cotton put down his vial and his syringe. 'Look, lady, you want to, you take this man away. He can ride over to Vegas – or any place else you want. Find someone with a fancy qualification. Doubt he'd last the ride, mind. The man's dying.'

At this Mr Baker gave a hoarse groan. His eyes rolled over the doctor and then onto me, where they stopped. The look he gave me was chilling.

'Leave me in peace,' he said. 'I haven't got long.'

'This won't do, Mr Baker,' Aunt Hilda said. 'We have got to get you to a proper doctor.'

'There is nothing any doctor can do.'

'A proper doctor. A surgeon.' She turned to Doc Cotton. 'Surely there is a qualified doctor somewhere near here?'

He shrugged. 'Maybe a day's ride.'

'We must send for him at once,' Aunt Hilda said.

But Mr Baker seemed to have found some reserves of strength.

'I order you to leave me . . . GO!'

'You're in no fit state to make that decision.'

'Miss Salter . . . leave me. I must talk to your niece.'

'Shush now.

'JUST GET THE HELL OUT OF HERE!' he shouted.

Mr Baker had used all his strength to sit up, the veins standing out in his neck. It was awful, the elderly, half-naked man sitting there propped on one trembling arm, his face red with rage.

'I am going to die now,' he said in a quieter voice, 'but first I want to have one last talk with Kit. In private.'

'GO!' I hissed, anger rising in me. 'Respect him, will you?'

'I think we should do as she says,' said Rachel softly. 'It's Mr Baker's wish.'

'I will be calling the *real* doctor. This man is sick and in no position to know his own mind.' With that Aunt Hilda sailed out, the others trailing behind her. Waldo turned to me and smiled, as if we liked each other. As if we even *knew* each other. I gave an icy glare to the air above his head. Then finally they were all gone, even the enthusiastic veterinarian and his assistant. I was left alone with Mr Baker.

I brought him a pillow to sit him up against the wall, averting my eyes from his sad, shrunken body. The vial of his blood was on top of the cabinet with the animal bones. Would Doc Cotton even have known the first thing to do in Baker's case?

Mr Baker held out his hand. I knew he wanted me to take it, though he'd never made such a gesture to me before. I reached out and took it in mine, feeling the thinness of his bones. There was nothing there. It was like cradling a dying sparrow.

'I'm going to hell,' he said.

'Don't—'

'Stop trying to be kind. I deserve all the torments of the damned – but before I go I need to tell—'

'You don't,' I interrupted. 'You don't need to say anything.'

'Oh yes, I do . . . I need to tell you the truth.'

'You've told me the truth.'

'No, Kit, not all of it.'

❧ Chapter Twenty-two ❧

'It's hard,' Mr Baker said. 'I don't know where to begin.'

'Then, please . . . don't talk.'

He looked at me, his gaze watery. Something in there was sharp though, as if he guessed at my fears. Guessed that I didn't want him to talk – didn't really wish to know any more awful truths. I let his hand drop. There was a small, hard object in my palm, which I looked at dully. My mind was far away.

'We can just sit here quietly,' I said.

'I haven't got long. I've got to tell you. I'm dying. It is now or never.'

All this talk of death was making me uncomfortable. He didn't *know*. How could anyone know they were to die?

'Rest. If anything is going to make you better, it is peace and quiet,' I murmured.

'No. You deserve more.' He paused and drew another shuddering breath. 'Understand this, Kit. I never told you the one important thing. It's all about Tabby.'

A jolt of something like fear made my body go rigid. I

didn't move a muscle. Since he'd said it in the desert, that name had been constantly in my thoughts.

'Ta . . .' I began slowly.

'Tabby. Tabitha. Your mother. You never really knew her.'

'Oh yes, I did. I was seven, nearly eight, when she—'

'A child.'

He drew in a deep breath, making a visible effort. I could see the muscles of his chest contracting and the tendons in his neck standing out. It made the speckled black snake, above his heart, move like oil on water.

My mother. What did this man have to do with my mother? Her smiling presence. Her vivid eyes. I never thought of my mother, tried not to, because it all came back to the same thing. She was gone. Would always be gone.

'My brother and I grew up near Huntsham, on Exmoor,' Mr Baker continued. 'A lonely place. Bleak, windswept, home only to heather and lichen. Our father was a servant, a butler, at the big house on the hill. Can you imagine the life of a servant? I believe not.'

'Of course I can. I've met—'

'Oh no, I don't think you could. Not really imagine it. Not really inhabit a servant's soul. You see, Kit, you are different to me. It was all given to you – the house in Oxford, the servants, the carriage.'

'We're not rich. We don't have a carriage,' I interrupted. 'Or servants. Apart from Mrs—'

He talked over me: 'For my brother and I, one emotion dominated everything. Envy. We used to visit the kitchens sometimes when the family was away. They were like palaces compared to our home. The shining silver, the fine bone china. I remember I left a smudge on a plate and my father told me off. Shouted. I couldn't believe it. The wealth, the ease, the lovely things. Then and there I vowed I would have it all – and more. My brother felt the same way, because, of course, we were as one.

'We wanted it. All of it. Money, horses, lovely things. We wanted footmen bowing as we entered our mansion. Elegant ladies hanging on our every word. But how were we to get it? As the children of the footman, who later became the butler, we were tolerated about the place. But there was an unbridgeable gulf between us and them.

'Us and them. We were beneath them, you see. Even when Tabby played chase with us through the stables and hay barns, we always knew that she was above us. She denied it, of course – Tabitha was a hothead – but we *knew*.'

'You knew my mother? As a child?' I broke in.

'Of course. Aren't you listening? We were best friends. Playmates. Cecil hoped for more. He was violently in love with her – but she laughed him off.'

'That was nothing to do with – you know – that Cecil

was the son of a butler,' I said. 'I know my mother was from a wealthy family, but she married my father, for heaven's sake. He's not a millionaire – or anything like it. She obviously just didn't like your brother – no offence meant.'

He looked at me – a smile twitching his lips. 'None taken.'

'I just doubt if a man like your brother was the kind of person someone like my mother would fall in love with. It's not a snobbish thing. Even if he was the son of a duke!'

'Cecil didn't see it that way. He believed it was his position in the world that made her reject him. And he never forgave Tabitha. He threw himself into money – and made a mint of it. And then when we were rich – very, very rich – he came back for Tabitha.'

'When was this?' I asked, speaking past the lump in my throat.

'Oh – she was married, if that's what you're enquiring about. You were just a little thing. We kept tabs on all that . . . Well, I won't go into exactly what Cecil did. Suffice to say, he was thorough about the thing. He saw hypnotists, criminals, sorcerers – all sorts of practitioners of the dark arts. Finally he found a very old and extremely evil Frenchman who had dabbled in witchcraft and alchemy. *He hoped to use the dark arts to win her forever.*

'The plan went wrong. And your mother died.'

184

'She died in an accident. That's what I was always told.'

'That's what they said. It was all hushed up. Your father went a little mad after her death. We kept tabs on that too. And Cecil decided that if he couldn't have your mother he would have you.'

I drew back from the table, shrinking away from the sight of this wretched man. This pale sack of decaying flesh. He thought it was fine to talk like this. About killing my mother – and wanting me, in some strange way, in her place.

Cyril was looking up at the ceiling now, away from me. He was talking to himself. 'You see, once he had all the money in the world, Cecil became concerned for his soul. He decided he needed *you*.'

'What did he need from *me*?'

'Your soul, Kit. It was Tabby's daughter's soul he craved.'

'So . . .' I paused and drew breath. 'That's why you – and your brother – never had me killed? I was useful to you?' I found my voice had risen in my indignation.

A strangled laugh escaped from Baker's throat. 'My dear, it took considerable self-control for Cecil not to kill you. The temptation was fairly strong sometimes. Not to mention your friends. I personally had to intervene several times to stop him having Waldo quietly knifed.

'For some reason, Waldo particularly got on his nerves.

There's his youth, his looks – and you must admit he's rather arrogant.'

I wasn't really listening. I was too shocked by what Cyril Baker had just told me. About the repulsive twins having been my mother's childhood playmates. About my mother, lovely, headstrong, dead – unwittingly behind their hideous schemes for money and power. So Cecil Baker had killed my mother, and now he wanted me. I was caught like a bug in a sticky web of witchcraft.

My whole being cried out against it. But at some deep level it all made sense. Why had the Bakers always been so interested in me? Not in lovely Rachel, or Waldo, or Isaac. It was always *me*. Now Cecil Baker was stalking me, with the snake of death gliding up my arm, towards my heart.

I can't pretend my thoughts were clear. My head was spinning with it all. The other objects that Baker had sought: the Egyptian book of immense antiquity; the sacred waters of Shambala in the Himalayas, which he believed would bring him immortality and which instead had cursed him; the bones of the sage in China. Now this.

He had lost those other treasures; did he hope to make it all up by finding this sacred Anasazi tablet?

Why? What did he hope to achieve? But I was strong. I would fight him with all I had.

'I am scared for you, Kit,' Cyril rasped. 'I've been

thinking it over. You shouldn't go to the Grand Canyon. What he plans there—'

'I am not afraid of death,' I interrupted.

He gave a cracked laugh. 'Death? You think it's your death I'm frightened of? What my brother plans for you, *dear* Kit, is far, far worse than death.'

⁓⊙⁓

Silence hung between us for a bit as I brooded on his words. My mother. Something worse than death. The Grand Canyon.

I looked down at him, my gaze arrested by the snake moving over his chest. It had stopped. Its head had disappeared, as if it had begun to burrow downwards.

The snake had begun its descent to Baker's heart.

'The snake?' I asked. 'What is it?'

His eyes locked on mine. They had a faraway look, as if they were gazing beyond me, Kit, to something only *he* could see.

'Don't you understand?'

'No.'

'The snake is the disease in our souls. I am marked, as are you and my brother, Cecil. It is all the ugliness, the greed, the envy, the desire for more and more and more. The waters of eternal life in Shambala created this grub of sickness. Eventually it came to the surface of our skin, a

187

foul snake. Oh, why didn't we listen to the guardian of that mountain paradise? She said we shouldn't drink, that we shouldn't even be there. But we paid her no heed. Now the snake searches for a way back in.'

'Back in?' I echoed, my voice quavering.

The long speech had exhausted Baker. He collapsed and stared at the ceiling. 'Back into our heart,' he said, finally. 'It's rather ironic, Kit, for, you see, the Black Snake is also the name Cecil gave to our organisation. Not the official one that handles our business affairs, but the secret society dedicated to the dark arts.'

His breathing was shallow and furious, the red patches on his pale cheeks crude daubs, like the make-up of a clown. His eyes roved around the room for a while, as if he was seeking something, and I let him be, brooding on what he had said. Black snakes. Snakes crawling up the skin. Black snakes in the land of the white sun.

'Kit!' Baker's voice was panicky as he reached up to clutch me. 'Don't let my brother have my body. Make him leave it alone.'

'What can you mean?'

Baker's lashes fluttered, his pale eyes burrowing, like a snake, into mine.

'Bury me. No burn me. As quick as you can. Tomorrow. No—'

'You're going to be well. Please, Cyril . . .'

But his hand dropped away, sudden as a stone. The agonising movement of his chest slowed, then ceased.

His eyes were still locked on mine. Even from beyond, they were holding me to account.

I leaned over to him and gently closed his lashes. To my surprise my eyes were wet.

Just at that moment, as I felt his skin burning under my hands, Aunt Hilda came bounding through the door. 'It's all arranged,' she boomed. 'We've got a stagecoach to take Baker to Chloride City and then, if need be, on to Vegas, if there's no help to be had there. We're going to . . .' She stopped mid-sentence as her eye fell on Cyril's body.

'Oh – I see I am too—'

'Yes, Aunt Hilda, you're too late. Cyril Baker is dead.'

❧ Chapter Twenty-three ❧

We were a sad group that night. We gathered in Aunt Hilda's room in Red Dobie's boarding house-cum-salon. The tinkle of the music-hall piano downstairs, the clang of metal pitchers and the occasional wild burst of laughter came through the floor. We didn't feel much like laughing; melancholy claimed us. We sat in silence.

It is sad to lose a friend. Even though Mr Baker had been the strangest friend I'd ever had. It had taken a long time for me to learn to like him. Even in the desert, riding our stagecoach or tramping for miles on foot, there had been something that lingered in the back of my mind. Mistrust. I couldn't forget that this was a man who had lied and cheated and murdered, who had traded in human beings as if they were so many pieces on a chessboard. But then, slowly, flashes of real generosity from him had put me to shame. *It is possible for someone to change.* He had offered me his last sugar-coated wafer. Made me swap seats in the stagecoach, so I could rest my head against the side window.

These generosities sound small, but there was also the larger thing. That he had gone against his brother, who by the sound of it had always dominated him. He had cast off evil and stood up, at last, for the right thing. Now that he was dead, I finally realised how much I valued his loyalty, how much safer he made us all feel. He had died so far from home, without his brother, who for most of his life had been everything to him. My heart was heavy as lead.

They planned to bury him in the camp's cemetery; it had taken a furious argument on my part for them to agree to burn his body first. I shuddered to think what Cyril was afraid of. Cecil was versed in the dark arts – who knew what diabolical uses he could have for his brother's body?

I had told my friends a little of what he said as he lay dying, though not all. Aunt Hilda paced up and down the small room, her boots thudding on the bare planks. Frankly her restlessness was getting on my nerves. Now she broke the silence.

'We're jammered,' she said.

'Pardon?' Rachel said.

'Word I made up, pretty obvious really. We're in a jam. Or in a pickle, a stew, a soup. A big juicy jam. Up the creek without a paddle, stuck in the Irrawaddy in monsoon, canoeing down the Thames in a leaky—'

'We get the point,' Waldo cut in.

She flashed him a smile. Waldo was always her favourite.

If Rachel had interrupted her, it would have been another story.

'Cards on the table?' Aunt Hilda continued. 'As far as I can see, we're stuck in this godforsaken place in the middle of nowhere. We don't know where we are going, because Mr Baker was leading us on this foolish wild-goose chase. And, to cap it all, we are stone-cold broke. Not a nickel or a dime to our name. So far Red Dobie, who I must say seems a bit of a gentleman, is footing the bill. But how long before he turns off the tap?'

'Pretty soon, I should think,' Waldo said. 'It's every man for himself out here.'

'Exactly. And in normal circs I heartily approve. But these aren't normal, blast it!' Her eyes gleamed. 'If it comes to it, we might have to put Rebecca here to work as a showgirl.'

Rachel blinked, then flushed deep red. Isaac let out a brotherly yelp of outrage.

'What?' Aunt Hilda said innocently. 'I'm only saying that she's a pretty little thing. These miners would pay a good deal to hear her sing. Let's face it – we don't have many options. The way things stand at present, we don't even have enough to pay our stagecoach back to civilisation.'

'Things haven't come to such a pass,' I said, quietly. I dug into my pocket and lifted something out. Then I strode over to the side of the room and held the thing to the lamp. It was a big stone, the size of a sparrow's egg, and it shone with a million points of blue light. How it blazed! It was by far the brightest thing in that shabby hotel room.

A chorus of *ooh*s and *aah*s came from my friends.

'It's beautiful!' Rachel gasped, looking at it greedily. 'I've never seen something so lovely.'

Aunt Hilda strode forward and lifted it out of my hand. She held it between her stubby fingers, tilting it this way and that so that it caught the light. The stone sparkled, warming my aunt's face.

'An Indian diamond. From one of the Raj's princely states, if I'm not mistaken. And of darn good quality. Where on earth did you get it, Kit?'

'You'd have to ask Mr Baker. My guess is that the brothers bought it, or stole it, when they were in India. He pressed it on me when he was dying. Said he'd hidden it in the false bottom of his trunk. Bandit Bart had emptied the trunk, but didn't think of a false bottom. It wasn't till later, after he had died, that I looked at it and realised how fine it was.'

'I'm not surprised,' Waldo said. 'A man like that. A millionaire. He would have carried some insurance on him. Well – thank heavens he was so practical. One has to have an instinct for saving one's skin.'

I gave Waldo a hard look. I hadn't forgotten what he had done to our Apache friends. Everything about him was repulsive to me. His slick blond hair, the look of smugness about his full lips, his self-satisfied blue eyes.

'Oh, I expect *you* know all about being practical, Waldo,' I said. 'It's all about Number One with you, isn't it? Blast the consequences for anyone else.'

I felt a moment of glorious satisfaction as I saw the look of shock on his face. Aunt Hilda turned round and glared at me.

'Well, I think Waldo has the right attitude,' she snapped. 'We have to be sensible here.'

'Oh, don't you worry. I won't let the side down. I'll be just as selfish as you and Waldo,' I snapped at Aunt Hilda, and stalked out of the room.

⚬⚭⚬

The air was blue with smoke in the saloon bar downstairs and thick with conversation. The others hurried after me as I entered the room. A cowboy was tinkling away at an out-of-tune piano, and a couple of showgirls were dancing. They wore ruffled scarlet skirts, scandalously short for they only just covered their knees. They kicked their legs in the air to reveal lacy white underwear. Their hair was bright blonde and they had thick circles of rouge on their cheeks. A third lady was singing, or at least that's what I think she was doing. Her voice was so whiskey-rough it wouldn't have disgraced a gunslinger.

Rachel coughed as we entered the saloon. I could tell she didn't want to be here. Aunt Hilda strode forward, though, cutting her way through the throng of cowboys, miners and the men playing poker in a cloud of cigarette smoke. I noticed the card players had a beautiful cover on the table. It was made of soft skin and sewn with intricate blue beads. Unmistakably an Apache tunic. It must have been a trophy from their raid on our friends' village. The sight made me harden my heart even more against my former friend Waldo.

There weren't many women here, to be sure, a handful apart from the saloon girls, but that didn't bother my aunt. You had to admire her. Whether at a garden party at Buckingham Palace or at a raucous bar in the middle of nowhere, she was always precisely the same.

'What's your best whiskey?' she barked to the bartender. The sea of revellers parted for her, as if she was Queen Victoria herself. 'The very best, mind.'

'I guess that would be Red Eye or maybe Coffin Juice,' the bartender replied.

'Ha! I'll have a double Coffin Juice and, let me see, lemonade for the—'

'I'll have a beer,' Waldo said, puffing out his chest.

I glanced at him. Here he was again, showing off that he was older than the rest of us. By one measly year.

'Very well, a beer and three lemonades.'

The bartender returned in a few minutes with the three cold glasses of lemon, the beer and the whiskey.

'That'll be fifty cents,' he mumbled.

'I'm afraid I can't pay,' my aunt bellowed at the top of her voice.

'Ma'am?' the bartender mumbled, confused.

'Drat it, man, can't you speak English? We're flat broke. We were robbed and we simply have no money left.'

Why my aunt chose to boom this embarrassing information so loudly I had no idea. The tinkling piano stopped and every head turned to us, so it seemed. I flushed red and I could see Waldo was mortified. He cares so much about appearances. And, of course, he pretends he is an American now. Down the bar, Red Dobie, who was drinking a flagon of ale with a girl on his arm, turned to us, frowning. I wondered why Aunt Hilda was testing his patience so much. He had been generous, for he was grateful for the return of his horse Carlito. But, as she had already warned us, there were limits!

'Put it on the tab,' Red Dobie yelled. He paused and his lips curled. 'This time.'

Aunt Hilda had the attention of every man and woman in the room. She smiled, enjoying herself.

'I haven't been quite clear,' she said. 'I should have said, we can't pay with money.'

Out of her bag she drew the diamond and held it up, in the centre of her flat palm. We were in the middle of a crowded saloon, blazing with gaslight, glittering with glasses, chandeliers and the showgirls' cheap jewellery. It wasn't the dingy bedroom upstairs.

Yet the purity of that diamond's glow, its intense blue flame, drew every eye in the room. A silence grew and Aunt Hilda, every inch the showman, let it linger for a while.

'This,' she said, 'is no ordinary diamond. It is a fabled gem. Priceless and unique. Ladies and gentlemen, you see here before you – all the way from the savage shores of the Hindu Kush – the incomparable Gem of Jaipur!'

A deep *oooh* went around the room. The pretty red-haired girl on Dobie's arm, in what looked like a corset and a tiered skirt, was staring hungrily at the gem.

'As you may have heard,' Aunt Hilda continued, 'we are travellers from far away. From good old England. While we were guests in your fine country, one of your fellows robbed us. He took everything we owned, practically down to our gold teeth!

'This isn't what I call hospitality, but we'll skate over that. We were penniless, desperate. If it hadn't been for Red over here, we would have starved. Thank you, Mr Dobie, by the way.'

Red gave a little bow as all eyes turned to him. Aunt Hilda continued, in full sail.

'We would be in a pretty pickle right now if it wasn't for one thing. One of my friends, Mr Cyril Baker, God rest his soul, was clever. Oh yes, he was clever enough to hide the Gem of Jaipur from the robbers.

'So, I offer this gem to you tonight for auction. Only dire circumstances would force me to sell it, but as you have heard, our situation is truly desperate.

'Now, lords, ladies and gentleman,' Aunt Hilda said, getting carried away, for there were no lords and few gentlemen for miles, 'THE GEM OF JAIPUR GOES TO THE HIGHEST BIDDER TONIGHT.'

She stopped and closed her hand, cutting off the diamond from general view. Then she sank down onto a barstool. With her left hand, she picked up the glass of whiskey and downed it in one gulp. An admiring buzz filled the bar.

Red Dobie's girl turned towards him and cried, 'I got to have that diamond, Red. If you love me, if you truly love me . . .'

'Now listen here, sweetie,' Red said, licking his lips nervously, 'be sensible, cutie pie.'

'Don't cutie pie me. I tell you I want that Gem of Jedburgh, or whatever it is.'

Other drinkers, the more prosperous-looking, were also staring greedily at my aunt. But she took her time, clicking her fingers for more whiskey, which she downed equally quickly. I hoped she wouldn't be too drunk to auction the diamond.

'Right,' she said, getting up off the stool and revealing

the diamond in her hand. 'I am going to start the bidding at one thousand dollars.'

There was a huge gasp around the saloon bar. Red paled. Aunt Hilda frowned in irritation.

'I call that a very, very fair starting price. Take this diamond into any jewellery store in New York or Frisco and you would get twenty times that sum, easy profits. How do you put it over here? Fast bucks, ladies and gentlemen.'

I had no doubt my aunt was telling the truth because the diamond looked rare and valuable. But this was a poor town in a rough desert. There were no pots of gold buried in these people's backyards, or so I would guess.

'So who'll be man enough to bid me a thousand dollars?'

To my surprise a dozen or so hands went up. Red Dobie's among them. It seemed I had underestimated the wealth in these parts. Perhaps there really was silver and gold buried in the desert around here, as well as lead and copper.

As Aunt Hilda led the bidding higher and higher, most of the bidders fell away. There were only a couple left now, Red Dobie and a man at the bar, whose mouth was shaped in a permanent sneer. He wore a ten-gallon cowboy hat and two nickel derringers on his belt. From the way people shrank from him, I guessed he was not popular – an outlaw maybe, or some kind of villain.

The bidding was up to five thousand dollars now. A lot of money, more money than many people would see in their lifetime. Aunt Hilda abruptly stopped at that. She turned to Dobie and Mr Sneer.

'You both desperate for this diamond, correct?'

'Give my last bullet for it,' said Mr Sneer.

'Yeah – we are,' Red muttered, with a glance at his girl.

'Then prove it. I've got all the money we need. In fact, I don't need to cart a great wad of dollars around. We'll only be robbed again. It's other stuff we want now. Horses, provisions, guns. I see the truth of it now: guns are more important than food in the Wild West.'

'We can give you all that,' said Dobie.

'We'll give you a share of the saloon, half of it,' said the girl, flouncing her skirts and shaking her glossy carrot hair at the same time.

'A tenth,' said Dobie.

'Red!' the girl snapped.

'Make it a quarter,' Dobie said.

'I'll take a tenth of your saloon,' said Aunt Hilda. 'It looks like a good business. I also need good horses for all my friends, provisions, and let's say a couple thousand dollars to see us through back to Frisco.'

'Done!' said Dobie, while the other man snarled, 'Not so fast. It ain't a fair bargain.'

A couple of derringers glinted in the gaslight, one for each hand. People screamed and backed against the saloon walls, others dived under the tables. In seconds a path had cleared between Dobie and Mr Sneer, both of them holding their pistols. My aunt was still there, sitting straight-backed at the bar, holding her glass of whiskey.

'Now don't be a fool, Jack,' Dobie drawled. 'You know I don't allow no gunfights in my saloon.'

'Seems to me that you gettin' some mighty preferential treatment, Red. I could stand it when it was just Candy here; she's a tramp anyway—'

'You take that back.' Red snarled at the insult to his girl.

For answer Mr Sneer raised his guns. But Red was quicker – his hands flashed: *bang, bang*. In a split second both pistols had been shot clean out of his opponent's hands. All that remained of them was smoking lumps of metal on the sawdust floor.

Pure fury glinted in Mr Sneer's eyes. He spat at Red, a huge gobbet of saliva, then turned tail and stormed out of the saloon. The doors swung after him, banging violently.

'Don't be coming back, Jack,' Red shouted. 'As sheriff, I say your sort are not wanted here. This is a decent law-abidin' town.'

'I'LL BE BACK,' came the yell through the saloon doors.

As soon as Jack, or Mr Sneer, as I thought of him, had gone, conversation started up again. The poker players went back to their tables, the girls flocked together, chattering excitedly. Shoot-outs, it seemed, were not that rare in this bar, whatever rules Red liked to lay down.

Waldo was whispering in my aunt's ear. She listened and then turned to Red with a big grin.

'Hey, Mr Dobie,' she yelled at the top of her voice. 'I forgot to say, we want one horse in particular – Carlito.'

A huge gasp went up around the saloon. I could see hard-bitten miners shaking their heads. Others started whispering. There was anguish on the face of Red Dobie; you could see him wrestling with the dilemma. His girl put her hand on his shoulder and turned him round to look in her eyes.

'For me, Red,' she said.

'All right – take him. Carlito's yours,' said Dobie. He blinked, his eyes watering.

I frowned at Aunt Hilda. I thought she was being cruel to Dobie, who after all had been kind enough to us. He had made a big mistake. Surely there were other girls in Chloride City? And beyond in Las Vegas and Dodge City? But there was only one Carlito. And I would take a horse over a diamond any day. A diamond is only a piece of rock, while a horse is a living, breathing treasure, one that can take you to the ends of the earth.

'A bottle of champagne to celebrate!' Aunt Hilda bellowed. 'I'm buying.'

'We don't have champagne,' said Dobie, who didn't look like celebrating at all.

'In that case, another whiskey for me. Beer on the house for everybody, Red, courtesy of me, Hilda Salter.'

Dozens of people descended on the bar. Some looked as if they hadn't washed for weeks. My aunt was hidden by a loud, drunken mass, and for a moment I thought they would lift her on their shoulders. Others began singing, 'For 'e's a jolly good fellow. . .'.

Apparently they believed Aunt Hilda was a man!

❧

So that is how we became part owners of one of the wildest saloon bars in the whole Wild West.

I'd thought of many outcomes for my journey – but not that we would become owners of what my father would have called a low drinking den! Well, you never can tell what life will hold, especially when you set off from the safety of your neighbourhood into the great wide world.

It was several hours before we were able to retire to bed. In that time, I think Aunt Hilda had stood half of Nevada strong liquor. We'd seen the showgirls dance the cancan – and left just before a drunken brawl looked likely to start up, for some of Mr Sneer's friends were in a very bad mood after he was denied the diamond.

I had seen enough of the West to guess that drunken brawls were usually resolved down the barrel of a gun.

❧ Chapter Twenty-four ❧

I awoke in the night, feeling uneasy. I was wearing a short-sleeved lace night dress, which Dobie had begged for me from one of the girls. It was scratchy and uncomfortable, and I was drenched in sweat. In the moonshine filtering through the shutters I could see the snake on my arm. It had been crawling upwards to my collar bone. But now, unless I was imagining it, it was moving diagonally. Towards my heart.

Perhaps Cyril's death had spurred it to move faster.

Dark horror descended on me.

Sure, Aunt Hilda had saved the day by auctioning the diamond. We now had enough money to get to the Grand Canyon. But where precisely? Where were we to go? The canyon covered miles of rocky chasms and raging rivers. Cyril Baker had been leading our trip, guided by some map of his own. Though we often worried we were heading into a trap, at least Cyril had known where we were going.

Now we were flailing in the darkness. A darkness inhabited by ghosts with the features of Cyril's evil twin.

I needed to use the toilet. Slipping my feet into some borrowed slippers, I padded softly out of the room, so as not to wake Rachel, and onto the landing. The saloon bar was finally asleep, the whole hotel shrouded in silence. I blundered a little as there was no moonlight here, and bumped into a warm body.

Terrified, I let out a shriek.

'Whoa there! Where you going at this time of night?' a voice said.

For a moment I was thankful that it was only Waldo. Then I remembered and drew myself up stiffly.

'I might ask the same question of you,' I said.

'It was a call of nature,' Waldo replied.

'Likewise. If you'll stand aside, I'll be on my way.'

'What is the matter with you? You've been giving me the evil eye for the whole day.'

'You're imagining things. I never looked at you once.'

Waldo sighed and moved towards me. He smelt of sweat and wood smoke. I hastily moved away. I needed to remember that I hated him.

'Come on. Tell me – what is it that I'm supposed to have done?'

All I wanted in the world was to be out of there, but the self-pity in his voice made me pause.

'You really don't know?'

'No, I really have no idea why you've been glaring at

me and jumping aside whenever I come near you. You're treating me like a leper.'

'Better a leper than a coward.'

'What?'

'You really, truly, have no idea what you've done?'

'NO! For heaven's sake, no. I already told you that.'

'Then you are even more boneheaded than I always thought.'

Our voices had risen in our anger. I saw a shadow slip out of one of the doors and realised we had company. No matter. Waldo's shame should be broadcast to the world.

'Just tell me.'

'Fine. Today in front of the whole of Chloride City you cast a few dozen people to the wolves. You did it casually, without a second's pity or reflection about the fate of those poor Apaches. Because of you, they will be hunted down – most probably be killed.' I halted for a second, the words choking in my throat. 'You might think they're just savages. But they were kind to us. They gave us food and shelter and horses. Saved our lives. And you repaid them by throwing away theirs. And you know what the worst part is?'

I paused to let him reply, but he was silent so I continued.

'The very worst part is *you*. Waldo Bell. A person so *heartless* that you didn't even *think* about condemning people to death.'

A lamp was flickering in front of the shadow. I saw it was Rachel. The light danced on Waldo's face. He looked furious. I expected Rachel to tell me off, but I didn't care. I didn't care if they all told me off. I knew we had been in a nasty hole, with the miners ready to skin us alive for stealing Carlito, but there was no need to sacrifice others to save our own skins. There must have been some other way out of the mess.

'Kit's right,' Rachel said quietly. 'You did a bad thing. I'm disappointed in you.'

Waldo's mouth opened then shut. I glanced at Rachel in surprise. She was quiet, but very angry.

'Aren't you going to say anything?' I said. 'I thought you'd have had some neat justification ready.'

'Look here, you've got it all wrong. I didn't give the settlers the right directions.'

I glanced at Rachel and saw that she was as unconvinced as I was. We had both heard his excellent, precise directions.

'As I thought. A nice, neat justification all wrapped up in ribbons and—'

'I'm going back to bed,' Rachel interrupted. 'I suggest you do the same.'

Without another word I sidestepped Waldo and made my way downstairs.

Most of the town turned out the next day for Cyril Baker's funeral. Hundreds of people – men, women and a few children dressed in shabby black and sweltering under the fierce sun. I guess any diversion was rare here. Even the funeral of a stranger they had never known was some entertainment. We made a strange sight, here in the desert, surrounded by sand, rocks and cacti.

This was one of the cemeteries known as a 'boothill' because it contained so many who had died unexpectedly – with their boots on. Many graves were little more than mounds of stones, with weathered planks nailed into crosses above them. My eyes wandered over the inscriptions on the makeshift crosses as the mourners gathered and the preacher in white robes stood at the foot of the funeral pyre.

Here lies MO. He took four slugs from a .44 . . . Buckskin Joe shot by One-Eye Walt . . . Rock Johnson. Very Dead . . . It took three six shooters to Kill Charlie Pinkett. He was dragged here by a cowboy with a rope around his feet.

The saddest epitaphs were the shortest. The ones with just a plank of wood stuck into a heap of stones and the legend *'Unknown'*. I think the only happy man in that cemetery was *'Smiley Johnson'*, who was unusual enough to have *'Died of Natural Causes'*.

'People have such short lives out here,' murmured Waldo, who was standing next to Isaac and me. It was true

– it was rare to see the grave of a man who had lived to his fifties.

I turned away coldly and saw Isaac flash me a look of surprise. No matter, it would all be out in the open soon. In fact, the sooner I told everyone how I felt about Waldo, the better.

The preacher began intoning the funeral service. He had an odd rasping voice, and stopped for breath between each sentence. It made his address even more haunting as he spoke about sin, and our friend who was being burned today, who had committed many grave crimes against God. But he had seen the error of his ways in his last days and repented and sought Jesus's love.

The preacher only hoped that Mr Cyril Baker had done enough to save himself from the fiery furnaces raging below ground. He painted a vivid picture of hell, the never-ending torments handed out to those who had lived an evil life.

The townsfolk listened respectfully with several interjecting 'Praise the Lord' here and there. Some of them were probably here because they hoped Aunt Hilda would buy them more drinks later. She was becoming a bit of a local legend.

Then the service was over and the match was put to the funeral pyre. We watched it burn, the smoke rising black and oily for a bit. Then my aunt and Waldo, surrounded by admirers, went to make their way back into town.

I drew my aunt to one side and said I needed a private word. This was going to be hard; Aunt Hilda had always had a soft spot for Waldo.

'I think it would be better if Waldo went back to San Francisco and we continued the rest of the journey without him,' I said.

'Why on earth would we want to lose Waldo?'

'We can't trust him.'

'He's a darn good fighter. The best shot we've got.' She corrected herself: 'After me, of course.'

'Aunt Hilda, he isn't honest – or to be depended on.'

'What's this? Another of your lovers' tiffs?'

I sighed. 'We're not lovers and this isn't a tiff. If you must know, I detest the way he betrayed the Apaches. Even *you* must have noticed. He told those cowboys right out where to find them. I cannot continue to put my trust in someone who could behave like that.'

'Stuff and nonsense.' Aunt Hilda smirked at me. 'You do get the craziest notions in your head.' Raising her voice, she yahooed to Waldo who was striding ahead with a party, including Red Dobie and his pretty girl. The girl was awfully friendly with Waldo, I noticed. Well, she could have him.

'Hey, Waldo, c'm'ere.'

'What is it?' Waldo called, turning round.

'My niece wants you to go back to Frisco!' Aunt Hilda bellowed.

A hurt look passed over Waldo's face. Serve him right. Half the mourning party had turned too, to witness our quarrel.

'This isn't the time, Hilda,' I hissed angrily. 'You go on. I need a moment.'

Hilda groaned and stomped away.

I purposely dawdled, desperate to get rid of the others. I needed a moment's peace. A black mood was upon me. The quarrel with Waldo. The feeling of being utterly lost, of flailing in the dark, with hidden forces opposing us. The reverend's sermon had affected me powerfully too. Maybe it was the desert sun, but I could feel the heat of that hellfire on my skin. I lingered and slipped further and further behind the others, dwelling on my own errors.

I had the same mortal illness as Cyril Baker. I could feel it eating away at my mind, wriggling on my skin. If I was to die soon, would I go to hell?

My thoughts were interrupted by a loud hissing.

'*Pssst!*'

Startled, I looked to the left and right. There was no one to be seen near me. Just the dwindling desert, scrub and prickly bushes. In front, mourners were heading down the path, back into town.

'Kit Salter – here.'

The voice seemed to be coming from ground level. I stooped down near a thorny mesquite bush and saw a pair of gleaming black eyes fixed on me.

'Do not be afraid.'

It was Boy, my crazy Apache friend, her face smeared with red clay, her black hair caked with dust. She was lying flat on her tummy, wearing nothing except her short deerskin tunic. Unbelievably, she was grinning at me.

'Me afraid? If the settlers catch you, Boy, they'll have your guts.'

'They will never catch me.'

'They know you stole Carlito.'

'What is Carlito?'

'Rolling Thunder – the most wonderful horse in the West.'

'Ah yes, he is mine. I will take him back.'

'He is not yours. He belongs to Red Dobie. You stole him.' I corrected myself. 'He belongs to Aunt Hilda now – but still you mustn't steal, Boy – they will hang you for it.'

From ahead, Isaac looked back and shouted at me to hurry up.

'Coming,' I called back, then turned to Boy.

'I must go. You too. Go now, Boy. It is too dangerous for you here.'

212

'I come to warn you of danger. Far-Seeing Man, he tell me that your friend, the pale ghost, he is dead.'

'How did he know?' I gasped.

'Far-Seeing Man knows all. This is why he named Far-Seeing Man.'

'Far-Seeing Man must have known Cyril couldn't survive his illness.'

'I tell you, he *sees*. *Also he sees that you are in the dark.*'

I drew a deep breath, because this was exactly how I had been feeling.

'You are running in the dark and have nowhere to go. So Far-Seeing Man sends me to guide you to light. I will take you to the Grand Canyon.'

I wanted to pour out my thanks, to weep almost, but I bit them down. 'How will you know where to take us?'

'I will follow Far-Seeing Man's steps. Tomorrow at first light take the road south out of this place and ride for ten thousand paces on the desert road, just between those two mountains.' From her position on the sand Boy pointed the way. 'Then you will come to a rock shaped like a horsehead. There I will meet you and take you onwards.'

'We will be there,' I said. 'Boy – I don't know how to say it – thank you.'

Boy grinned at me. I noticed there was a new gap between her front teeth, right in the middle. She must have lost a tooth in a fight. The sight sent a pang of fear through me.

'Your village. The . . . the other Apaches. They are not taken . . . They are safe?' Fear and guilt made me stumble over my words, which were like bitter lumps in my mouth.

'What do you mean?'

'There are not too many dead?'

'Why dead?'

'But the settlers . . . They came and raided you. I saw that tunic they captured. The beaded one. I saw them set off – Boy, I must tell you this: it is our fault.'

Boy laughed. 'The settlers came – I was hiding in the trees, watching with the braves. They cursed and cursed when they found out we had gone. There was nothing for them – nothing but that tunic. We left them that as it was an unclean thing. The woman who wore it is gone to Usen.'

I stared at her. Usen, the Apache creator god. What sense did this make?

'But, Kit, you know this all. I told it to your friend Yellow Hair. I say, if you are stuck, tell them the way to our village. We will be long gone. They can never find us.'

'KIT SALTER!' my aunt boomed. 'What in heaven's name are you doing out there? Come on right now.'

With a hurried farewell to my Apache friend, I rejoined the rest of the mourners.

❧ Chapter Twenty-five ❧

The wake for Cyril Baker was in full swing by the time I arrived at the Last-Dance Saloon. The atmosphere was more like a drunken party than a funeral. The piano player was banging away at a lively tune, the girls were dancing in a froth of bare ankles and scarlet skirts, Aunt Hilda was standing drinks all round.

It was only just noon and she was already knocking back the Coffin Juice. Her cheeks were flushed and she had a hectic glitter in her eyes.

Waldo was talking to Red's girl, whose name, it turned out, was Candy. Candy, for pity's sake. She might as well have called herself Strawberry Tart or Lemon Sherbet. Waldo was drinking beer with a manly air. Rachel and Isaac both looked a bit uncomfortable, nursing their lemonades in another corner of the bar. I noticed a handsome young cowboy was leaning over Rachel, smiling. Her face, however, was set.

As soon as she saw me, she made an excuse and left him. Isaac followed her.

'Thank goodness you rescued me,' she hissed. 'That cowboy hasn't had a bath for a month. He stank!'

'He was talking about what a good life the frontier wife has,' Isaac grinned.

'I can just see you knee-deep in cowboy babies, all wearing ten-gallon hats,' I said, smiling at Rachel. She didn't smile back but changed the subject:

'We need to get your aunt out of here. She's tipsy. She's going to make a fool of herself.'

'Before lunch!' Isaac said, as if that was especially scandalous.

'She's old enough to look after herself,' I replied. 'Anyway, I know from experience that no one can handle alcohol like Aunt Hilda. She must have some sort of well inside her where it all goes.'

Waldo caught sight of us at that moment. With a sort of smirk he bent down and whispered something in Candy's ear. She was tossing her red curls and smiling up at Waldo, just as if he was a big piece of strawberry pie. I felt uneasy. Boy had made it clear that I had misjudged Waldo. Not that I cared, but he was being an idiot. Red Dobie looked none too happy about him being so friendly to his girl. After all, the saloon keeper had given away his favourite horse just so the silly girl could have the biggest diamond in the Wild West.

Well, I could have warned him. There was only one Carlito.

Aunt Hilda caught sight of me. 'Come over here, Kit,' she bellowed, beckoning me vigorously.

I made my way through the noise, the smoke, the miners, cowboys, gunslingers and handfuls of saloon girls to Aunt Hilda. Didn't anyone do any work in Chloride City? I had several knocks by the time I'd barged through to her.

She introduced me to Red. 'My niece, Kit.'

'We've already met,' I reminded her.

'One of the finest girls in England. Brave, loyal to a fault. Not much to look at, I know, but then nor am I.'

I caught a glimpse of myself in the mirror behind the bar. I was sunburnt, unwashed and my hair was wild.

'Aunt Hilda, have you gone mad?' I snapped. I kept a straight face, but inside I was hurt. I may not be a beauty like Rachel, but I am not unpleasing-looking.

'I mean, she's fine-looking, of course, as any niece of mine would be – just not a mimsy-wimsy beauty type. Why, Kit can fire a gun better than any man. She's a credit to me.'

'I'm sure she is,' Red Dobie said, his eyes twinkling.

'Where is this going, Aunt?' I enquired coldly. 'Have you discussed the arrangements for tomorrow? We really should be getting on, you know.'

'Slow down. I've been talking all that over with Red here. Provisions, water, directions.'

'We'll do everything to help, ma'am,' Red said.

'Red is being remarkably helpful,' Aunt Hilda said, gazing at him flirtatiously. 'Anyone would think he was keen to see the last of us.'

'Not me, ma'am,' Red protested, but I was sure he would be – especially Waldo, and Aunt Hilda was being a right nuisance too.

'Could we take lunch in your room?' I suggested to Aunt Hilda. 'We could plan our trip over it and then buy the necessary provisions in the afternoon.'

Was it my imagination or was Aunt Hilda becoming a little sweet on Red Dobie? Or maybe she just wanted to sink her hooks into her investment in the Last-Dance Saloon. Either way, it was a relief to get her up to the bedroom, and for the steaming urn of soup to arrive. None too soon, for, unusually, I was starving.

The soup was thin and had pig's trotters floating in it. Revolting. I had no time to fuss, for as soon as we sat down to eat at the little round table by the window Waldo stood up again.

'I have an announcement to make,' he said. 'This will come as no surprise to some of you. Others, I hope, will regret what I have to say.'

'Oh, do sit down,' Aunt Hilda said. 'This delicious soup will get cold if we have to listen to you jabbering.'

'No. I must speak my mind. I have decided not to join

218

you on your trip to the Grand Canyon. I will take the first available stagecoach back to San Francisco.' He paused. When he spoke again, there was a catch to his voice. 'I will not rejoin you on the journey back to England. I intend to telegraph my mother and tell her I am staying on in America.' He raised his blond head proudly. 'I will seek my fortune out here.'

There was a shocked silence. Rachel threw me an uneasy glance, but didn't say anything. Then Isaac began to protest:

'We're a team, Waldo. I have the ideas and you do the fighting. Why would you want to leave? We work brilliantly together.' His voice rose. 'I don't understand why you would abandon us.'

'Ask Kit,' Waldo said.

I was looking at the floor and didn't raise my eyes to meet his.

'Go on, ask her.'

'Kit?' Isaac said.

'Look, this is all stuff and nonsense,' Aunt Hilda interrupted. 'A silly tiff. You're not leaving us, Waldo. I won't allow it.'

I cleared my throat. 'I'm truly sorry, Waldo,' I said. 'I misjudged you. You did not betray the Apaches – I had the wrong idea – but if you want to leave you must do as you please.'

Waldo gave a nasty laugh. 'That's just like you, Kit. You say you're sorry but in the same breath you take it away. You say I must leave.'

I hadn't said that, but I resisted pointing it out. Instead I forced contrite words out. 'Please stay. I would prefer it.'

'Prefer it?' Waldo rose from the table. 'Too little, too late. I'm sick and tired of you throwing your weight around. Treating me like the dirt under your heel . . . I'm sorry, I'm very fond of you, Kit, but I just can't abide it any longer.'

Rachel's low voice broke into this exchange. 'This is between the two of you,' she said. 'I must say, I think you're being silly and melodramatic, Waldo.' She turned to me. 'Kit, what I don't understand is this: how do you know that Waldo didn't betray the Apaches?'

I explained about meeting Boy after the funeral, and how she had told me that the Apaches were safe, that Waldo had known they were moving camp. My words caused a sensation, for the others marvelled at the daring of the Apache maiden to come within shooting distance of Chloride. I think Waldo was perhaps a little upset that his sensational statement had been upstaged.

'So,' I said, 'I was wrong. I flew off the handle. I should have known better. Waldo, please forgive me and come with us.'

I looked him in the eye as I said this. The most humbling apology I have ever had to make to him. He looked at me, and his eyes were distant, hooded by his frowning brows.

'I've been really upset.'

'I know.'

'I can't decide now. I'll think about it and let you know tomorrow morning.'

'Oh, stop being such a *girl*,' Aunt Hilda butted in. 'We can't do without you. For one thing, Kit's father already thinks you let her down in China. He would never forgive you if you jumped ship now. For another, this is no pleasure trip we're setting out on. It is a life-and-death matter for my niece. If you leave us now, you're abandoning Kit and betraying the rest of us. So, it's settled. You're coming with us.'

That for Aunt Hilda was that. But from the look on Waldo's face I wouldn't bet on her getting her way.

❧ Chapter Twenty-six ❧

We assembled just after daybreak in the spiky shade of a pinyon pine. There wasn't a cloud in the sky, just flat blue that threatened to whiten till it burned with a dazzling heat. Another roasting day in the desert. Riding for miles, with aching limbs and the sun frying our brains through our straw hats.

I wasn't exactly looking forward to it.

Nor was anyone else, if the glum faces of our party were a guide.

Aunt Hilda had obtained a new outfit, and had a pair of fringed leather trousers to go with her ten-gallon hat. She looked weird, frankly, but then she never cares what anyone else thinks about her. Seeing her stomping about, ordering people around, getting the horses ready, packing provisions in the saddlebags, I wondered again if she ever regretted her lost opportunity for love with Gaston Champlon.

When I say we were all gathered for our departure from Chloride, I should say everyone except Waldo. It took my aunt a while to notice his absence.

'Where is that dratted boy?' she asked. 'Kit, run up to his room and find him. He's holding us all up.'

'I'd rather not,' I said.

Red Dobie, who had come to see we had everything we needed, offered to do it himself. But Aunt Hilda sent Isaac. Both of them came down from the saloon a while later, a forlorn Isaac dragging a sullen Waldo behind him.

'Well, what's going on?' Aunt Hilda said.

Waldo didn't reply, just looked mulish.

'I don't think he's coming,' said Rachel.

'WHAT?' Aunt Hilda exploded. 'Of all the childish, ridiculous pranks to pull! I do not believe it of you, Waldo Bell. I've always had a lot of time for you, and I simply don't believe you would let your team down like this. Kit is mortally sick, for pity's sake.'

'I have no choice,' Waldo muttered. 'Kit has made it clear she doesn't want me.'

'Absolute nonsense. My niece may have a sharp tongue, but she apologised – very handsomely. It is you who is being childish and stupid. There, I've said it. Frankly, you are being ridiculous.'

'I'm sorry you feel that way.'

'Get on your horse now.'

'NO!'

'Waldo, I command you.'

'There isn't a stagecoach till next week so I'm going to ride to Las Vegas and get one from there.'

'FOR—' Aunt Hilda was puce-faced, building up to a major explosion. Though I was angry, hurt even, I kept my temper. If Waldo wanted to go, fine, he must.

'Aunt,' I cut in, 'I think we should respect Waldo's wishes.' I glanced at Candy, Red Dobie's girl, who had also turned up to wish us goodbye. 'It may be that he finds the amenities of Chloride too much to leave.'

Waldo looked at me as if he wanted to kill me.

'We should waste no more time,' I declared, putting my foot into the stirrup and hoisting myself onto Carlito. 'The sun will be scorching soon; we must move if we want to avoid the heat of the day.

So we left Chloride and left Waldo. I resisted looking back to see his dwindling figure standing under the pines as we rode out. Maybe he stood there watching us ride into the horizon. Or maybe he turned as soon as the dust had settled, and went back into the Last-Dance Saloon for a beer and a consoling chat with Candy.

Either way, I didn't want to waste time thinking about it.

⁂

We followed the directions Boy had given us, riding due south out of Chloride. It was strange not having Cyril guiding us. I felt freer without his gloomy presence, but also a little adrift. He had led us, I realised now. We had been following his path and his plans.

Now we were riding on a whim – the chance that we would meet Boy and she would somehow give us the guidance we sought. We had no choice, because we had so little idea of our mission – just that we had to get to the Grand Canyon to seek the legendary tablet, the thing we hoped would free me from my illness. I had seen Cyril die; I had felt the presence of his brother. I was in no doubt about the urgency of our quest. If we didn't find this Anasazi tablet, this thing of sacred antiquity, I would face certain doom.

Isaac was riding beside me, unusually quiet even for him. Abruptly he said, 'You've made a big mistake.'

'Pardon?'

'Waldo puts up with you. There won't be many that will.'

'I cannot see that this is your concern,' I said, glancing ahead to see Rachel riding silently beside my aunt.

'I'm your friend. I'm also Waldo's friend. I can understand why he acted as he did. You are in the wrong. You should have gone down on bended knee and begged for his forgiveness.'

'Thank you for sharing your opinions,' I said, spurring Carlito on with my stirrups. There was a sour taste in my mouth. I set my head away from him so he could not see my flaming cheeks.

It was just before noon when we came to the rock shaped like a horse. It was a large boulder and it did look uncannily like Carlito's head. The left side of it took the shape of a muzzle. I could see the flare of the horse's nostril in a bit of chipped stone.

Boy was sitting on the sand in the shade of the rock. She must have been there for hours. She was so still that at first I didn't notice her. Her deerskin tunic blended with the colours of sand and rock.

'I have joy to see you, Kit,' she said, standing up. Her chopped hair, black and straight, framed her lively, intelligent face. Her eyes were gleaming, her full mouth opened wide in a smile.

I jumped off my horse and was just about to fling my arms around her neck when I remembered that Apaches don't like such displays of emotion.

'Friends of Kit, welcome,' she greeted the others. 'But Yellow Hair – he has been shot?'

I guess it is natural in this violent land to always dread death by the bullet. I quickly assured her that Waldo was fine, had just decided to stay behind.

'A pity,' she said. 'He is a fine warrior.'

We broke our ride then, to rest a little in the shade of the rock, to eat some dried beef and have a drink of water.

The sun was overhead, beating down on us with fury. We all huddled into the sparse shade of the rock. Then it was time to go. Boy wanted to make good progress towards the canyon before we made camp for the night.

It was a relief to my wounded soul to have her with us. She seemed to anticipate what I was thinking, understand when I was weak or my head was filled with that odd combination of burning and dizzying lightness. Most of her attention was turned on me; she gave Rachel, Isaac and Aunt Hilda just politeness. To me, she was constantly kind. I didn't know why she was so – perhaps she had been charged by her shaman to look after me and was taking her task very seriously.

And, of course, we were friends. She had been raised in a wickiup, a creature of the burning deserts. I had lived in a cream stucco house in Oxford with a governess and table manners. But somehow we understood each other.

'Boy,' I asked her once, 'is it unusual for an Apache girl to be a warrior?'

She glanced at me, her eyes shining with amusement. 'There is no shame in taking another path.'

I blushed. 'Doesn't it make you feel rather, I don't know, different?'

'But I am different.'

'I know – but all the normal things. You know, getting married?'

227

'These things are not for me.'

'Isn't there someone you *like*?'

'I have told you – this is not my way.'

The look she gave me as she said this was intense. Remembering her tragic story, all the death and destruction she had seen, I took her at her word. Anyway, she was right. Why does every girl need to go down the same path? Some English ladies are explorers, like my aunt. Though not many, I admit. I could see that Boy, with her wild hair, strong limbs and fierce spirit, was unique.

Proud and free and untamed.

So we rode across the desert, through sand and rock and the strange prickly Joshua trees, towards the craggy mountains. Several times I had the feeling, looking back, of a malevolent presence following us. A shadow, a darting figure, a startled bird. I wondered about Cecil Baker. Even more since Cyril's death I had come to feel his presence all around. In the glare of a desert fox, or the shadow of a vulture wheeling far above us in the burning sky. Where was he now? What was he planning?

My mind was on these things, not really on the desert around me. Apaches find beauty in the desolation, but I felt only bleakness. I was tired of riding, of the weakness in my body. Cyril's death had made me feel frailer than ever.

That is my excuse, anyway. I was in a fog, not really paying attention to my mount, even though we were racing along at a fair clip. Then Carlito stumbled. I found myself flying sideways, my left leg caught in the stirrup. I would have tumbled to the ground, bashing my head and possibly breaking my leg, if Boy, with stunning swiftness, had not leaned over and caught me.

'You fool of a girl,' Aunt Hilda yelled at me. 'Your head is so full of Waldo you're not paying the slightest attention to your horse.'

I had *not* been thinking of Waldo, and was going to say so, but Boy interrupted and shushed my aunt. I could see that she was very angry as she leaped off her own horse and went over to Carlito. The animal was very distressed, his sweaty flanks heaving, his eyes rolling. At first it seemed as if he was lamed, but luckily it was only that a thorn from one of the spiky cacti had caught in his shoe. Boy managed to remove it, then gently she comforted him, feeding him a handful of something, which was clearly a treat, for the horse gulped it down.

'Rolling Thunder needs rest,' Boy said. 'You will ride with me. He will come by our side.'

I agreed readily enough. The fall had shaken me and I felt nervous about controlling the huge black stallion. I could see that Boy understood and commanded him in a way I did not. Anyway, I was tired and it comforted me to ride behind my friend, to feel her, warm and confident, in front of me.

I realised that Boy was taking care of me, that it was not just for Carlito's sake that she had made me ride with her.

The mountains rose abruptly in fantastical broken shapes from the edge of the desert. They looked like shattered toys, as if some god had hurled them down in a fit of rage. We rode up a perilous cliff path. As the sun was setting, in a wash of scarlet that made the whole land glow with fiery heat, Boy said we would make camp for the night. We had no tents to put up, so we simply gathered a few fragments of scrubby bush and thorn in a hollow and made a makeshift fire. In our one cooking pot Boy brewed up a stew made of mutton, wild sage, roots and sharp-tasting red berries she had gathered. We ate it out of our tin cups, spooning the slush straight into our mouths. It was delicious.

There was a nip in the air. We were all thankful that Red Dobie had packed us blankets. We rolled ourselves up in them and lay by the fire, listening to Boy's tales of the old Apache ways.

We believe that the Indians are heathens; certainly they are less sophisticated than us. They have not invented guns and railways and telegraphs and other modern marvels. But the way she spoke of their union with nature, how they lived in harmony with the spirits of tree and bird, of coyote, elk and bear, made me believe that they possess a deep wisdom. A wisdom, perhaps, that is lost to us.

Boy told us how the Indians believe that we were not put on Earth to shape it to our will, to make great cities rise from the desert. Instead, they believe, we are just a speck in an endless natural flow. This includes not just all *living* things, the swallow above and the worm underfoot, but the great Earth itself. And the clouds drifting through the sky and the rain they bring.

Even Aunt Hilda listened in a sort of trance, for Boy's voice was low and lilting, as natural and soothing as a breeze. I fell asleep with firelight glinting red in my eyes, warmed by the stories of ancient gods.

❧

I awoke with a start, a great wrenching lunge. There was screaming all around me, the frantic neighing of horses. I was colder than I have ever been in my life. My hands were icy, my lungs freezing, my eyes rimed in frost.

Where was I? Who was I? Just chill in my bones and the deathly, glacial heart of a creature who does not care for a living thing.

I looked down. There was a knife in my right hand. It was covered in blood. I was bleeding. All around me were the coal-black shapes of the horses, stark against the murk of dawn.

I knelt down. Slowly my hand moved upwards to slash at the horse's flank. I lusted to hurt. To wound. I craved the beast's howl of agony. All I knew was the knife, heavy in my hands, gleaming dully.

Carlito shrieked, neighing, jerking at his rope. A shot rang out. A shot out of nowhere. I jerked, and fell to the ground, veins pulsing, head throbbing, flesh tingling.

'What the blazes?' Aunt Hilda was towering over me, looking in horror at the bloody knife in my hand. 'Kit. What in heaven's name are you doing?'

'I-I . . .' A stutter came out of my mouth.

Carlito, a cut in his glossy black flank. Warm blood pouring out of it. Whinnying in pain.

'I don't know.' I began to cry. Tears streamed down my face. Great juddering sobs coughed up from my lungs. 'Please.' I looked at the knife in my hand and couldn't begin to understand what it was doing there.

'You hurt Carlito. You were trying to lame him,' Isaac wailed. 'I saw you.'

'No,' Rachel said. She was just rising from her blankets. 'Kit would never do that.'

'I saw her. I woke up and saw Kit was over there and I was going to say something. But then she had the knife and I saw she'd cut Carlito and I was so horrified I couldn't . . .' Isaac said, in one long, agonised breath.

'That is not Kit.' Boy had appeared in our midst, her

232

copper face shining with certainty. 'She was possessed. It was the skinwalker who attacked Rolling Thunder.'

'The skinwalker?' I gasped. I felt like retching. Intense pain seared my arm where the snake glided. I was shivering, trembling uncontrollably. The knife slipped from my grasp and fell to the ground. My knees were too weak to hold me.

'You were possessed. This I truly believe.' Boy looked down at the frothing Carlito, neighing in agony from his cut. The anger stood out on her face. 'To hurt a horse like Rolling Thunder. A perfect animal.' She paused, looked at me. 'If that shot had not come – it broke you from your possession. If . . .'

'Thank you,' Aunt Hilda said to Boy. 'You saved her.'

'No. It wasn't me.'

We looked at each other. Five faces in a ring, alarm and horror stark on all.

'If it wasn't you, Boy,' Aunt Hilda said, 'who was it?'

Then, from the darkness, another shot rang out.

A single loud bang.

'Who did that?' Rachel shrieked.

None of us had fired it. The bullet had come from behind me.

Someone was watching us. Out there in the darkness someone was stalking us.

There was a silence. Cecil, the skinwalker. The evil

magus. It must have been him. An unseen presence, creeping after us, following every move. We had guessed at him in the boarding house. Sensed him trailing us. But why would he want to shock me out of my trance if he was possessing me?

More to the point, was he still out there?

'Who is it?' Boy asked, drawing her pistol. 'Show yourself.'

A tall figure stepped out of the shadows into the candlelight.

'It was me,' a cold voice said. 'I saw it all.'

❧ Chapter Twenty-seven ❧

Waldo stood there on the edge of our camp in a new canvas jacket and denim trousers, a bandolier of bullets slung over his shoulder. His clothes were dusty and stained, the hand which clasped his pistol filthy. He wore a wide-brimmed cowboy hat, which threw the top of his face into shade so I could not see his eyes. I didn't dare guess their expression.

'Waldo!' Rachel gasped, and, running to him, threw her arms about his neck. 'Thank goodness it's you.'

'What are you doing here?' I blurted.

'That's not much of a thank-you for saving Carlito.' Aunt Hilda embraced him too.

Everyone crowded around Waldo, dragging him to the centre of the camp. Rachel had forgotten her earlier criticisms of him, as had Aunt Hilda. It was only Boy and I who stood slightly to one side.

'Are you hungry?' Aunt Hilda asked. 'Let's start the fire and make you a cup of tea.'

Boy and Isaac were set to the task. It was still night,

perhaps about four o'clock, more than an hour before the sun would rise, so we were moving in murky darkness. But no one felt like going back to sleep. A fire was lit, water was boiled, tea was made. We drank it with slices of stale bread smeared with lard. When this was gone, our supply of bread would be finished.

'I saw it all,' said Waldo, after he'd drunk a mug of strong, sweet tea. 'Something made me wake up and I came to the edge of the camp. Kit, you were walking. You walked straight past me. Your eyes were open but you were not *seeing*.' He paused. 'I'd never seen you look like that. Your eyes did not look normal. There was nothing there. They were cold and dead. I've never seen another creature like that, let alone you.'

I shuddered because I had seen such eyes before. On the deer that had invaded the Apache village.

'Then you went to the horses. You walked past Rhino and Jango. You went to Carlito. I saw you were holding a knife. That one with the mother-of-pearl handle. You stooped down and cut Carlito with it, very deliberately in his side. That's when I fired the first shot.'

'It woke me up!' Isaac said, staring hard at me. 'I saw you too.'

'Then you bent down. I fired another shot. You seemed to shake then – and . . .'

'You saved her,' Boy said softly. 'Yellow Hair, you

236

saved your friend. You shocked the skinwalker out of her soul.'

I breathed deeply and then took a long gulp of the sweet tea. It was all very well Boy talking about the skinwalker, but I felt dirty. I had hurt Carlito. I could have lamed him. Destroyed him forever. It would be my hand, the evil in my heart. Never mind the force Boy believed had possessed me. Nothing inside *me* had resisted it.

I was corrupted by evil.

'Maybe we should change the subject,' Rachel said, glancing at me. 'Something more cheerful?'

'Hard to think of anything cheerful in this godfor-saken place.' Aunt Hilda waved her hand at the barren mountainside, tinted rose by the rising sun.

There was a melancholy silence, then Isaac spoke. 'You didn't answer Kit's question, you know,' he said to Waldo. 'What are you doing here?'

'The answer's obvious,' Waldo said, gazing in my direction.

'Of course it's obvious,' Aunt Hilda said. 'Waldo realised he simply couldn't abandon me.'

Waldo looked at Aunt Hilda and smiled. 'I guess that's it, ma'am,' he said.

'He couldn't keep away,' Aunt Hilda said. 'He realised I simply couldn't look after you all out here in the wilderness. We need more than one good shot.'

'Boy's a good shot,' I protested, 'and I am not bad.'

'Don't be ridiculous,' Aunt Hilda snapped. 'It's a great responsibility for me. Leading you out here in this place infested with bandits and savage Indians and skinwalkers and goodness knows what. I need someone by my side I can trust.'

Waldo wasn't listening. He had risen and, cradling the warm cup of tea between both hands, was moving restlessly around. Rachel and Isaac began arguing with my aunt, who didn't notice that she had insulted all Indians in front of Boy. Waldo came and squatted by my side.

'You know I didn't come back for your aunt,' he said, in an undertone.

My heart flipped over inside my chest. His eyes sought mine again, and he smiled.

'We both know your aunt can look after herself.'

Finding myself on surer ground, I grinned back at him. 'At least we agree on one thing.'

'Kit . . .' His smile was gone. 'If I'm to come back, things have to change.'

I found it impossible to speak.

'You must never, ever, treat me like that again.'

I was going to ask him what he meant. What was he thinking of, making demands of me in such a tone of voice? I'd made a mistake, but that didn't mean he could lord it over me for evermore. But the normal Kit seemed to have deserted me. So I lowered my head and said:

'Yes.'

⌒◯⌒

Once Waldo had rejoined us, we journeyed a further week till we came to the Grand Canyon, through wild landscapes populated only by Indians, or the occasional rancher or trading post. I will never forget my first sight of our destination. Boy had talked of the majesty of this place. She hadn't been able to do it justice. When we stood on the south rim of the Canyon de Chelly, I gasped in wonder. It was like staring down into the abyss. Massive pinnacles of pink rock rose up to meet us, like teeth guarding the jaws of the underworld. It was awe-inspiring to think that billions of years ago eruptions in the earth's crust had produced these giant ripples and folds.

I understood now why the Indians spoke of the 'Earth Surface World'. Down there below was another world, mysterious, wreathed in smoke and flame. We only saw the top layer of what was real.

The Hopi Indians say that the Grand Canyon is where humans emerged into this, the Fourth World. They call it the *sipapu*, the womb of the world. Staring down into dizzying vortices of rock, I could see how this strange land had inspired them.

'It's like huge pieces of Red Leicester,' Aunt Hilda said, staring down into the canyon.

'You mean *the cheese*?' I asked.

'Crumbled bits of cheese,' Aunt Hilda said.

'I hate cheese.'

Waldo laughed. We had all been silent for a few moments. Stunned by the majesty of the canyon, humbled as we stood, mere ants, on its rim. But Aunt Hilda can puncture the most sacred feeling. She would stand at the gates of heaven and compare it to Blackpool.

The canyon dropped down, thousands of feet down, down, down to a glinting river. You could see flashes of greenery at the bottom. Boy had told me that the Indians had planted hundreds of peach trees, but the orchards had been destroyed by American soldiers.

If you lost your foothold on a loose stone, you would thud from boulder to boulder till your mangled body ended up in the Little Colorado River far down below.

'We must leave the horses here,' said Boy, with a worried look at the sky above. Storm clouds were massing, dark and thunderous. 'They will find food. Usen willing, we will meet them when we return.'

If we return, I thought as we set our steeds free with a swift pat on their flanks. It was an especial wrench for me to see Carlito go. Whenever I looked at him, at his fine,

240

glossy black flanks and the scar where I had wounded him, I felt deeply ashamed.

'I'll go first,' Aunt Hilda said, looking down the gut-churning chasm. 'Watch your step as you follow!'

'Please,' Boy said, nudging Aunt Hilda aside, 'I must lead.'

'But I've climbed all over the world,' Aunt Hilda protested. 'Blast it, I was a terror in the Himalayas.'

'This is a sacred trail,' Boy explained. 'It is secret. I must ask the spirits for their permission as we go down.' She pointed to the little leather pouch she wore about her neck. I knew she carried sacred pollen, which she scattered at holy places. 'I must seek their blessings.'

Aunt Hilda was about to argue, but a flash of Boy's dark eyes silenced her. The first section, plunging down from the trailhead, was a sheer wall of rock ending at a narrow ledge below. I would have thought it impassable, but Boy took it deftly, moving between tiny footholds in the surface. My heart beating with trepidation, I followed the blaze of her scarlet headband and glossy black hair. I couldn't help feeling scared, here, so close to our journey's end.

The presence of Cecil Baker hung over us. I sensed an attack in every hovering hawk, every scuttling lizard. The skinwalker was watching us. When would he make his move?

We all made it down to the ledge in one piece. My knees

and hands were scraped from contact with sharp rocks, my breath ragged. Sweat poured down my face. Even Aunt Hilda was a little less keen to lead after that ordeal, and we had only just begun our trek. It would be another seven or eight hours before we would reach the bottom of the canyon.

From the ledge we found a narrow trail. Boy blessed the beginning of it with pollen and we scrambled after her. The rock was not just pink; it was streaked with all sorts of colours from white to the red of iron ore. Ruins dotted the cliffs, the caved-in rock dwellings of humans who had lived here more than two thousand years ago. Their strange hieroglyphs could be seen etched on the walls, especially the hunchbacked flute player they called Kokopelli.

The presence of these ancient ghosts wrought feverish images in my mind. I could feel that we were nearing the end of our quest, but still had only vague ideas of what it was that we sought. An ancient Anasazi tablet, was all that I knew. One that had mystical powers – and that had been revered for centuries. One that the Hopi Indians believed had been given to them by their gods. But this was the nineteenth century. How could an ancient slab of stone help me?

'Boy,' I asked when we stopped for a sip of water after hiking for at least three hours, 'where are we going?'

'We go down,' she said, pointing to the shining river below.

'That much is obvious – then what?'

'There is a path. We must take it.'

'But, look, I'm confused. How do you know where?' I glanced around me. On every side there were canyons, gleaming cliffs of salmon-coloured rock. The roaring of the river, magnified by the echo chamber of cliffs, was pounding in my brain. 'I mean it's all just rock, rock, rock.'

'Not to me. Many of these places are sacred.'

I could have screamed in frustration. Where, exactly, were we going? What would we find there? She wouldn't tell me. It seemed as if she was being purposefully vague.

'But how do you know where to go?'

'Far-Seeing Man is guiding me.'

'Where? He isn't here. You have no map.'

'In my head. He guides me from the inside.'

With that I had to be content. It was another few hours before the vegetation thickened as we reached the bottom of the canyon. There were clumps of pinyon pines and juniper, feathery tamarisk trees, thorny bushes of prickly pear, snakeweed and sumac. The heat was increasing as we journeyed down. The air had that quality of stifling stillness which you experience before a storm. The sky was black and louring, thunderheads massing over the mesa far above.

'It looks like rain,' said Aunt Hilda.

'Yes,' said Boy.

'I suppose we can shelter in a cave.'

'It's dangerous. Waters come fast down the canyon.'

We had emerged from the trail by rapids that saw water tumbling and bouncing over boulders. The roar of water was bewildering, as were the croaking of frogs and the clouds of midges that hovered over our hands and faces. Skimming birds darted in and out of the mesquite and tamarisk. It was green, lush and hot, far hotter than the canyon's rim. I felt closer to the earth than ever before.

The river thrashed in both directions. I could see many turnings off from the path into smaller canyons and caves, the changing play of shadow and light, dark patches where centuries of water had worn into the cliffs. The sun was falling in the sky. Soon darkness would descend and we would be trapped here with the prowling canyon creatures – lynx, coyote and bear.

'Anyone want some beef jerky?' Waldo asked, after we had moistened our lips with water from our canteens. 'I still have a few strips—'

'Shush!' Boy cut him off, pointing to a large sandstone boulder.

From behind this rock, a snake slid into view. It was marked with brown circles on white and had a bulbous head and glaring eyes. My own snake brand, which had crawled up my arm to my throat gave me a twinge. As soon as it saw us, the snake made a loud rattling noise with its tail.

'A Mojave rattlesnake,' Isaac said, holding out his arms to shield Rachel.

'Stand aside,' Waldo said. He advanced towards the snake, a stout stick in his hand. 'I'm going to toss it into the river.'

'Wait!' hissed Boy. 'Stop.'

The snake had paused on the path and turned its head to look at Boy, almost with enquiry. Then with great speed it slithered off round the bend.

Boy looked at us for a moment, then disappeared after the snake.

I followed, running after her, my friends charging behind.

'Come back,' I hissed.

She paid no attention, following the snake, which was gliding, a flash of white and brown, down the track by the swollen, roaring river. I followed her as she followed the snake, alarm growing in my heart.

The snake slid off the path into a fissure of rock. Crouching down, Boy sped in its wake. I went after her, crawling through a tunnel. When I stood up, we were in a cave with weak shafts of light dotting the earthen floor. I could smell burning, and smoke wafted towards me.

The snake had disappeared. In its place stood a ferocious creature with a bloody mouth and eyes ringed with blue. A monster. It had transformed into a monster. Isaac screamed and Waldo, bellowing, raised his stick. Then I saw it was not a monster; it was a man wearing a wooden mask.

'Kit Salter,' a deep voice growled. Then one by one he called each of our party by name.

'Where is Far-Seeing Man?' Boy asked.

'He waits within. Follow me. I have something to show you.'

❧ Chapter Twenty-eight ❧

We followed the masked figure into the cave. My heart clenched inside my chest. Cold sweat stood out on my forehead. I felt my snake brand *move*. I could feel it gliding down, a slithery feeling like a wet finger travelling over my skin.

'Who are you?' Boy asked the figure.

'I am a Hopi shaman, a friend of Far-Seeing Man,' he replied.

We were in the cave now and could see the fire clearly. It was made of pinyon pine and brushwood, but there was something there that stank. A meaty smell that, as we came closer, made me want to gag. It was suffocating in the closeness of the cave.

'What is that?' Waldo gasped.

'A body,' Isaac said, his face white. 'Burning flesh.'

Something animal was in the fire, tatters of cream clothing shrivelling in the ashes. The gleam of white bones against the red of fire and coal.

I swayed a little and would have fallen, except Boy

caught me. Waldo let out an exclamation of shock as the Hopi shaman bent down and picked something up from the floor.

A small pink thing, with a gleam of gold about it.

He handed it to me and I backed away in horror, stumbling into Boy.

It was a human finger. Cut off just below the second joint. I could see the clean, polished nail, the trimmed cuticle and the heavy pillbox ring that circled the horrible thing.

It was a beautiful ring: 22-carat gold, with a white gold inlay of a snake circling a tiny box. The lid could be opened and used to store a lethal cyanide pill. It was ornate, yet discreet enough to pass unnoticed on the wearer's finger.

I had seen the twin of this ring before. Heard the cry of agony as it had been ripped from the owner's fingers.

'That's Cyril's ring,' Aunt Hilda cried out. 'Cyril Baker's.'

'No, Aunt Hilda,' I said. 'It's Cecil's.'

'But I saw Bandit Bart steal it from Cyril when we were held up.'

'He told me about it. They had identical rings made, with pillboxes in them. Each ring had a poison pill in it.'

Aunt Hilda stared at the burning corpse. 'So that must be—'

'Yes, Cecil's body.'

Isaac made an awful groaning sound and fled from

beside me. He stumbled to the side of the cave where he retched, while Rachel hastened to his side. I was aware of the silence hanging heavy as we watched our enemy's body sizzle with a terrible rancid crackling.

I would not have wished such a fate on anybody. Even a man with no heart.

'How did it happen?' I asked the Hopi shaman. 'Did you kill him?'

'No,' he replied. 'He was not clean. He was full of evil. He tried to go to the cavern of the ancestors and take the tablet. This tablet was given to us by our gods – so he was struck down.'

We stared at the flaming bundle, appalled. We should have rejoiced. In life Cecil was a cruel man. We had been terrified he would get here before us and use the tablet for awful ends. But death is a great leveller. It is the end of sin. It makes compassion, even for great wickedness, bloom in your heart. Here especially, where the Indians believe the skin between the worlds is thin as tissue. Where sorcery glows strong. Our enemy was dead; we were free of the evil that hung, like a hurricane cloud, over our heads. Free of the skinwalker who had tried so often to invade my mind, who had made me commit the worst crime of my life when I'd cut my innocent, perfect horse, Carlito.

He was dead. And yet there was no joy in our hearts. It

was too macabre, the burning body in this foetid hole of a cave.

'May we go to the cavern of the ancestors?' Aunt Hilda asked the shaman. 'I would very much like to see this tablet.'

I glanced at her, then looked away. It was too naked, her greed for possession of the sacred thing.

'How do we know that we will not be struck down like Cecil?' Waldo said. 'I don't—'

'You are right,' Boy interrupted. 'We must clean ourselves.' She pointed to two tiny huts, which stood near the far wall of the cave. They had been constructed out of bent willow saplings, covered with skins and blankets – and looked barely big enough for a dwarf.

'What are they?' Rachel asked.

'The shaman has built two medicine lodges,' Boy explained. 'There is one for women and one for men because they must not mix. We must perform the medicine before we go in search of the sacred tablet.'

'What?!' Rachel said.

Aunt Hilda stepped in. 'Keep your voice down, Rebecca,' she said. 'Indians believe that sweat ceremonies cleanse the evil before meeting spirits. Or some such. You clean your soul by sweating out all the badness, is that not right?' she demanded of Boy.

Boy nodded.

'It is an important ritual in these parts,' she explained. 'We must strip down and sweat out the bad in those huts.'

'Naked?' Rachel asked. 'Not naked?'

'Of course naked. That's why there are separate huts for men and women. Better get on. It's an interesting ritual, and I hear it can be quite pleasant,' Aunt Hilda said.

The rest of us were outraged, Waldo's chin jutting forward in a growl. There was something repulsive about the idea of sweating, naked, here in the bowels of the earth with Cecil Baker's body burning so near us.

'No,' I said. 'I'm sorry. I can't do it.'

The others were adding their protests to mine. Boy held up a slim hand.

'We must do this,' she said. 'If we do not do this, the shaman cannot take us to the cavern of the ancestors.

'This means we will not find the tablet.'

✦

Several hours of sweating later and my head felt as if it was floating off my body. My throat was parched, as Boy allowed only very few sips of water. The hot stones glowed in the centre of our sweat house, steam pouring off them. Boy chanted and drummed, her incantations whirling in my head. Occasionally she would take her buffalo horn

251

and pour more water on the glowing stones. Even more occasionally she would replace the stones with those from the fire blazing in the cave outside.

It was already hot in the canyon outside. In here it was hot, hot, hot.

My insides felt as if they had been opened and flayed by the burning stones. All the flesh was gone, shrivelled away. There wasn't anything left of me, just baking flesh. Somewhere very small inside was a shining nugget. It was *me*, Kit Salter.

I will not dwell on the sight of my aunt. She seemed quite at home naked, squatting in the heat like a giant toad. It was much more pleasant to avert my eyes. I will say, though, that the drumming and chanting made it all seem like a dream.

Boy was outside, gathering more hot stones, when Aunt Hilda turned to Rachel and me. Through the steam her face was contorted.

'I've just realised what this is,' she said.

'A steam bath,' I replied.

'It's a ritual. They are purifying us.'

'So?'

'You know what that means.'

'Of course,' I said. 'Cleansing our spirit and so on. The steam hissing up is the universe's creative fire.'

'No. *They're purifying us.* Rebecca, Kit, listen – perhaps

the Apaches purify people before they offer them as a sacrifice.'

'I don't understand.'

'A human sacrifice. To their gods.'

I didn't believe her. I couldn't believe her. Hadn't Boy and the shaman already shown they were on our side? And our enemy, Cecil Baker, was dead. But Aunt Hilda's words blended with the steam and the rhythmic chanting from the male sweat hut to create a terrifying din in my head.

Boy appeared, like a ghost, through the animal skins that formed the door of the sweat hut.

'We are ready for the cavern of the ancestors,' she said.

❧ Chapter Twenty-nine ❧

Boy, a splash of colour in her fawn dress and scarlet headband, stepped lightly across the earthen floor of the cave. We followed her, our tread heavy. The snake on my chest writhed, going in for the kill. Fear rose from my belly to meet it. What were we doing here? On a quest for some legendary tablet that we only knew of through rumour. A foolhardy mission led by Cyril Baker, a crazed man who was now dead. A dark foreboding hung over me. The 'Glittering World', the 'Earth Surface World', felt very far away. We were trapped here in the realm of shadow.

The shaman was waiting, along with Isaac and Waldo. His grotesque mask glowered at us in livid reds and blues. In the sweat hut I had asked Boy about the mask, and she'd said it was called a *kachina*. When he placed it on his head, a man *became* the supernatural spirit carved on the mask. *Kachina*s control the living – birds, beasts and humans – and can bring rain or sun. They were savage gods, it seemed to me.

Walking through the gloom, I realised that what I had

thought of as a cave was actually a natural drainage ditch. I could see a tiny patch of sky a mile above us. A glimpse of louring clouds. This cleft in the canyon had been caused by water pouring from the world above for time immemorial. I put out a hand to steady myself as, bending down, I followed Boy and the *kachina*.

Abruptly, as the sky far above our heads closed over into rock, we were plunged into darkness. My hand gripped the side of the tunnel, finding chill slimy stones, water-slick. Something clamped over my mouth and an iron grip took my other hand.

I tried to scream, but my voice was cut off by the leathery glove prodding into my mouth. My hands were tied, swiftly, before I had the chance to fight. I heard a shrill wail – Rachel. Then the sound of cursing – Waldo. Both of these noises were gone as quickly as they started, and in the damp silence I could only hear scuffling.

Something pushed me from behind and I stumbled onwards, almost falling into a large cavern. It was filled with watery light from far, far above. Too weak to dispel the gloom. Much stronger were the brands that flamed from pockets in the rock.

Rachel was flung down on the stony floor after me, then Waldo, Isaac, Aunt Hilda and Boy. All of them had their hands tied and were being shepherded by grotesque masked *kachina*s.

It was a nightmarish vision, the cavern rising like a gothic cathedral in a pointed star-shaped spire. Down on the floor, and in the rocky ledges to the sides, dozens of robed, feathered figures flitted. They leered at us, their gaudy faces covered with turquoise, yellow and orange masks. From the depths of the cavern a great drumming and chanting started up, and they began to dance.

In the blinking light of the flaming torches, I could distinguish a cavorting figure. Kokopelli, the humpbacked flute player, beloved of the ancient canyon dwellers. A sinister mud head, lumpish and coarse-featured, like a figure from a dream drawn by a four-year-old. A clown with huge, red, rubbery lips and sad black-rimmed eyes, half pathetic, half sinister.

One dancer, garbed in moccasins and a buckskin kilt, his body daubed with paint and adorned with beads and feathers, had a head shaped like a bluebottle. Black eyeholes were cut in his mask.

'Be calm,' said Boy, who was on her knees on the floor next to me, her hands bound behind her back. 'They will release us once they are sure we are pure.'

In the centre of the space a ledge of rock rose like an altar. It was made of dark, shiny basalt. It bore something propped upon a stand. It was hard to make out from this distance, but it looked to be of pink-veined marble, with figures that reminded me of Egyptian hieroglyphs inscribed on it.

'The tablet,' I said to Boy, while one of our captors poked me forward. 'Boy – that must be it. The Anasazi tablet.'

Wonder surged in me as I looked upon the thing. A slab of dull marble, not gold, not precious. But a thing of legend that for centuries people had fought and died over. A sacred object imbued with powers that were only talked of in hushed voices.

Aunt Hilda was staring at it, hunger on her face. I knew she would have given up any number of diamonds to possess this tablet. To return home to Oxford in triumph with this legendary stone, which the Indians claimed had been handed to them by their god.

She was not totally thoughtless, but at that moment she had forgotten that the tablet might actually cure me. All she saw was a picture of her everlasting fame as its discoverer.

'The Anasazi tablet,' she murmured in a trance. 'Boy, where is your master? We must be released. Where is Far-Seeing Man?'

'Far-Seeing Man is not coming back,' a voice behind us said.

The clown stepped out of the shadows, his rubbery face breaking into a smile.

'Far-Seeing Man is gone,' he said.

'What have you done to him?' Boy called, and the clown opened his mouth wide in a jangling laugh that echoed through the cavern.

'He is dead. Quite, quite dead. Your shaman is dead. Nah Kay Yen, the great far-seer, didn't see that, did he?'

↭ Chapter Thirty ↭

The clown was a slim figure with scarlet lips, and eyes that drooped at the side and drooled dark pus. It was wearing a black-and-white striped hat and had two horns growing from its head, tassels sprouting from the ends. More demon than jester, it struck dread into my heart.

'What are you?' asked Boy, recoiling from him as he leaped above her.

For answer the clown tossed away the watermelon that it was holding in its left hand and removed the striped leather glove. With horror I saw that the ring finger had been hacked away. In its place was a stub. A bloody, bandaged stub.

'Cecil Baker?' I groaned, staring at the diabolical mask.

'Clever, clever girl.' The clown cavorted over to me. 'Well, quite clever. I suppose I am the obvious suspect. Still, I knew I wasn't wrong. Cyril argued with me. Said you weren't worth it. But I always had faith in you.'

'It can't be. We saw your body . . . your finger,' Waldo cried. '*You are dead.*'

'But if I'm dead, how come I to stand before you now?'

'Your finger,' Aunt Hilda said. 'We saw your ring.'

'A clever trick.' His lips cleaved in delight. 'A genius trick, even if I say so myself.'

'If it is you, Cecil, show yourself,' I said, struggling to sit up. 'Prove this isn't just some horrible game.'

The clown's face split in a smile as big as a knife slash. 'My pleasure,' it said, and ripped off the mask.

Underneath, as ghastly as the clown's chalky mask, was Cecil. His eyes glittered with a manic glee, his tongue flickered like a lizard as he dropped down on his knees in front of me. The drumming increased in intensity and the dancers' feet pounded the rocks harder and harder.

'Never believe in half-truths,' he said loudly, spreading his hands out. '*Never see what you only desire to see.* The body you saw in the cave there was Far-Seeing Man. I had no more use for him, so I dressed him in my clothes and burned him.'

Boy exploded in screams.

'Your finger,' said Aunt Hilda. 'What happened to your finger?'

'I cut it off. A small price. I had no more use for it anyway.' As he said this, he waved his stumpy left hand, boasting of his madness. Then he dropped down close to me and began to speak in a low voice.

'I'm so glad,' Cecil whispered tenderly. 'Finally, after all

260

this time, you're mine.' He put out one hand and stroked my chest, where the snake's head was gliding downwards. Every inch of me recoiled in disgust from him, from his dead touch. It was like being embraced by a corpse.

He tore open his tunic to reveal a snake crawling towards his heart. A snake just like my own.

'See,' he said. 'We're not so different, after all. Only mine has such a damn grip that nothing will release it.'

'You deserve it.'

'Quite true. Perhaps you will have better luck.' He moved closer to me.

'Get away from me,' I spat.

'I don't think you quite understand,' he said. 'We will never be separated. Not now. You are the treasure I've been seeking. I've been dreaming of this moment half my life. Ever since your mother died.'

Never, ever, had I felt more hatred. Cecil must have seen what I felt. Briefly a shadow crossed his face, as if disappointed that I didn't share his rapture. Or was it possible he felt ashamed of what he was about to do? It was gone in an instant, replaced by the former wild glee. He jumped to his feet and, clicking his fingers, called his masked minions. Two of the Hopi Indian *kachina*s broke from the shadows and scurried over.

'They have betrayed us,' I whispered to Boy. 'Your Indian friends have betrayed us.'

Tears overflowed her eyes and rolled down her cheeks.

'Why did they do this? You always said the Hopi were the most peaceful of Indians. Why let this madman—'

My words were cut off as two Indians picked me up bodily. I struggled, fighting and kicking with all my might as they carried me over to the altar. It was no use; they were strong, their bodies hard. They swatted away my gouging fingernails and biting teeth as if they were the stings of a gnat.

Cecil Baker glided by me, murmuring into my ears: 'This tablet will make it all come true for me. I sought other objects of power: the waters in Tibet, the book in Egypt, the bones in China—'

'You lost them,' I spat.

'Who cares? This tablet exceeds them all in power. This prophecy rock is so powerful. Especially here, where the skin between the worlds is so thin. Like gossamer, like silk. So thin I can flick them apart and move between life and death.

'This tablet was given to the Hopi by their gods. It is as ancient as the canyon around us. Men crawled out of the earth here, dreaming of a higher world. It will give me the power I seek over life. It will make me complete – and you, Kit, are the heart of my plans.'

I turned my head away while he spoke, shutting out his insistent voice. I would not let it enter my ears and sully my thoughts. Then I had an idea. I raised my head and looked into his eyes.

'You do know, don't you, about your twin?'

'What of him?'

'Your brother, Cyril Baker. The only real love of your life.'

'That's not true. There were others – your mother.'

'Don't waste your breath on my mother. She had no time for you. No, the only person you ever cared for was your twin. You schemed together, grew rich together, your hearts beat together. And now –' I paused, letting the silence lengthen.

'Now he is dead,' Cecil said calmly. 'You cannot shock me. I knew it as soon as he passed.'

I took a deep breath. It seemed I could not disturb his manic composure. 'So, he is dead. He died in Chloride. He died dreading the hell he was doomed to, for all the things you did together.'

If the man had loved anyone, it was his brother, his twin. For a moment there was a spark of something in his pale eyes, some remnant of human emotion. Then they filmed over and there was nothing there. Once more they were empty. He clapped his hands and other gruesome *kachinas* picked up my friends, carrying them towards the basalt altar. I was laid upon the Anasazi tablet and my arms were untied. I tried stabbing into the masked eyes of the horned owl that was holding me, but I was too weak and too slow. With a shrill laugh the creature tied me to the tablet, passing the rope round my body and under the stone altar.

My friends, trussed up with willow cords and thick sisal, were flung at the base of the altar. There was no way out.

I turned my head sideways and began to pray that I would have the strength to escape from these bounds. The tablet was made of smooth marble, pinkish, white-veined, cold under my cheek. I could see gawky stick figures on it. Animals, birds, lightning, the sun. Petroglyphs of an immeasurably ancient civilisation.

Cecil's face loomed over me, rising up like a deformed crescent moon. His eyes were glazed over with pus, while his mouth moved. In the background the drumming and chanting reached a crescendo and sulphurous smoke began to coil round the altar, wrapping its way round my body, insinuating itself into my nose and up, dreamily, to my mind.

'Have no fear,' Cecil said. 'I'm not going to hurt you.'

Cold hands jerked the tablet away from under me, then laid it on my chest. It sizzled there, burning my skin as if it was a flaming branch. I felt the snake writhing under the tablet's power, diminishing. Inside my head I was screaming and screaming, but no sound came from my lips.

Abruptly, the drumming stilled. Cecil's hissing voice filled the silence.

'Is she ready?'

'Yes, master. The snake is gone.'

'Let me see. I want to see for myself.' A naked flame in the darkness . . . cold, rotting breath above me. 'Yes – you have done well.'

'Thank you, lord.'

'Very well.' His exultant voice filled my ears. 'The end of Cecil Baker begins.'

I knew then that the smoke was poison. The smell was bitter-sweet, lulling me to a drugged sleep. I knew I must not give in. *I must not close my eyes*, because if I did Cecil would destroy me. But there was something stronger than my will, the scent rank and rich. Not only in my nostrils, but seeping through my head. My lashes were so heavy I could not keep them open. Slowly they drooped – and closed.

The world went black.

❧ Chapter Thirty-one ❧

When I came to, there was a ringing in my ears. The cavern was pulsing with light pouring out of me, flowing straight and strong across the floor and up the walls. I saw everything, every rock, every mask, every feather. Each speck of dust was precise and purely drawn.

I had been untied. I stretched my arms, enjoying the power rippling through my young girl's muscles. I flexed my fingers, blinked, moved my fat tongue in my mouth. Slowly I uncoiled off the altar. A deep chill filled me, in my bones, my fingers, my eyes and my mind. I was so cold. Otherwise I had never felt better.

I was *alive*. The sentimentality, the emotions, that useless clutter that had clung to me like fog, were gone. I was able to look around, to view everything with a keen, calm vision. The chill was one of perfect logic, of sense unbound by feeling. Now, finally, I was ready to seize any opportunity. I glanced down at my chest and saw that the snake had disappeared. Gone, in a puff of smoke. Exultation filled me. The ritual of the sacred Anasazi tablet had worked. It had cleansed me of the evil snake brand. Now I was finally free and whole. No wonder I was so refreshed.

I was in charge now. Who am I? Why – it is plain for all to see. *Me, Kit Salter.*

Like a panther springing, I leaped off the altar and landed on the rock floor of the cavern.

I saw the face of the yellow-haired boy, his eyes wide with wonder and hope. I picked up the knife, the handle inlaid with turquoise stones, a silvery blade gleaming.

'Kit,' he said, 'they haven't harmed you?'

I stooped down and attacked his bonds. The knife slashed through willow and twine like cutting butter. Swiftly I freed the others: Hilda, Rachel, Isaac and Boy, the Indian squaw.

'What happened to Cecil Baker?' Hilda babbled. 'It was as if he suddenly had a fit. He hasn't moved. What's going on? Kit, tell me. Why did they let you go free?'

I glanced over to Cecil. He was standing frozen, his eyes glued to the altar. He was in a trance, bewitched. I looked away, trying to stop myself shuddering. He revolted me, the white, papery skin; the weak chin; narrow, drooping shoulders; the ugliness of his body. No wonder my beautiful mother, Tabitha, had rejected him.

Waldo rose and came towards me. His eyes were brimming over with some emotion I could not understand. Love. Yes, maybe it was love.

'Kit – dearest,' he said, holding out his arms to embrace me.

I moved towards him. 'I am not your dearest,' I replied, and thwacked him across the face. I heard the crunch of bone as my knuckle connected with his nose. Saw the shock on his face. The screams of the girl, Rachel. The bewilderment as Waldo put his hand to lip. But I had no time to dwell on his pain, enjoyable as it was.

'Take them to the altar,' I shouted to my people, and the *kachinas* swarmed from all corners of the cave to gather the human rubbish. That fat woman with the loud voice. The lanky boy in glasses, the Indian squaw, the other miserable children. The brown-haired girl was pretty, very pretty. Butterfly lashes. Eyes the colour of tea. I might have some use for her. But the rest of them . . . so much debris that I must dispose of in a sensible way. A way that will enhance my power.

The fat woman is gurgling at me: 'Kit, Kit, Kit! What's wrong with you?' I knock her over as I pass. She is old and ugly. Even worse than the children.

I am freezing. Cold to my very bones. I see clearly, but everything is rimed with frost.

'A blanket!' I call, and a *kachina* rushes to put a rug over my shoulders. From far above there is a giant rumble of thunder, the sound of the earth splitting open. The heavens cleave and a mighty gush of rain falls from the sky. My people are screaming, rushing around. But the water glances off me.

I am invincible.

This is the time to truly enjoy being me and to make my plans for the future. Not to be distracted by these annoying insects or the ice in my blood. As I pass the burning peyote tree, a whiff of strong smoke swirls up into my mind. Such sharp colours, such detail. The Anasazi tablet, patterned with creamy, pinkish veins and adorned with beautiful markings. What power it has given me.

My knife is smooth in my hand. It is a good knife, solid, the handle carved out of buffalo horn, the blade shining and polished. The feel of it pleases me. A *kachina* cowers as I pass him, knife in hand. Pleasure gusts through me. I have so many creatures. Buffalo, water maidens, warriors, clowns. So many souls bound to me. My slaves, my things. They feed into my power, making me swell with energy.

The time is near.

Soon it will be time for the final step.

Here in this cavern, deep in the greatest canyon in the world, the womb of the world, where humanity crawled on its belly out of the slime, I can feel the thinness of the ties that bind us to one world or another. I can feel the strength of my power to slip between souls, here with the rare air and the sacred smoke slipping into my lungs.

Who am *I*?

Well, I am no longer Cecil Baker; my need for that ugly old man is done. Now *I* am something far, far better. I am the skinwalker. I am the shaman. I am the thing that picks and chooses which body it shall use.

While I enjoy possession of this body, I am also Kit Salter. And I do enjoy it very much, the young body, the healthy mind. Yes, it is a strong vessel. I have chosen well.

It is clear to you, is it not? I, the skinwalker, have taken control of Kit Salter. Through the power of the Anasazi tablet, I have taken her body. Her soul, her weak, helpless soul, is gone, banished forever. I shall have no more trouble from *her*.

Yet what is this? Somewhere far away is a locked room. A small voice. It whines. I must pay it no attention.

'*You can do it, Kit,*' the voice cries. '*You can fight the monster.*'

Unbidden, an image flashes before me, the skinwalker. I sense that Kit's soul is seeing the same thing. An oval locket. A white blouse, a face engraved in the locket. Spirited eyes. Tabitha. They flash. They're signalling. But not to me. They are talking to that small voice in the locked room.

'*Fight, fight, don't give up, girl.*'

My mother. Her arms around me. Pushing me out of the cell where the skinwalker has imprisoned my soul. So much love in her touch. Love. I never knew the strength of her love.

She is pushing me and embracing me at the same time. She never gave up, so I must not.

Tabitha. Tabby. My mother. And now others join her. A whole chorus straining into that locked room. My father, Aunt Hilda, Waldo. Boy, her eyes full of tears.

'Don't give up. Get out, Kit. You're still there, fight him.'

But no. The old Kit is not here. Me, the skinwalker. I have her mind. The shaman. The person who used to be Cecil Baker.

This chorus inside me is nothing but an irritating mewl. I am stronger than these voices. The skinwalker is Kit Salter now. Her body is mine, and her soul. I will be Kit and thus I will escape hell and I will live forever. The tablet has cured me of the parasite inside me and the snake outside. I am strong and free.

And so young.

I have my whole life ahead of me. And then when I tire of Kit Salter . . . another body. Another ripe young body. It will be so easy.

'Conquer him, Kit. Pity him. Touch his heart.'

Not so easy. I have no heart. Still, I had better do it. Take that final step. Only sentimentality holds me back, and I have no time for feelings.

I glide over to the shell of Cecil Baker as he droops in front of the altar. I see with satisfaction that my people have tied up the intruders, piling them one on top of the other. The fat lady, Hilda Salter, is on the top of the pile. Ha! She will squash the rest of them.

Cecil stands there, frozen, gaping at them. How could I ever have called that body my own? He is repulsive. I collected beautiful things – just look at him! He was never much to look at! Why did I never leave that carcass before? I had the soul of an Apollo – was it fair that I was stuck with the body of a louse? Still, finally I have righted that error.

Better make it quick. I raise the knife, aiming for Cecil Baker's heart. When he is dead . . . Well, Cecil Baker will be dead forever and the skinwalker will be Kit Salter.

The knife is firm between my fingers. And then – *there it is again*! That same small voice . . .

'Pity him!'

Another soul, pure of heart, opposing me with all its might. And that chorus, urging the rebellious soul on.

'*You can do it, Kit. He knows nothing of life or love. He is already dead. Pity him.*'

I feel the opposition surging down my nerves into my fingertips. Like gas flaring, the strike of a match in darkness.

Panic takes over my mind. I must do it. I must do it now. Plunge the knife into the heart, feel the skin burst, the blood spurt. I must do it quick – or else . . .

I plant my will in my fist and bring the knife down onto the creature. Cecil doesn't flinch as the knife grazes his skin. I have a foretaste of victory coursing through my veins. So close! I am so close! Then that other will opposes me once again. The girl called Kit. We fight, silently, bitterly, over the knife. But she is not playing fair. She is not fighting; she is wrapping me in pity – and, worse than pity, love. She has learned to love Cyril, and through him – me.

Our souls collide in the knife, in the handle, the shimmering silver blade. There they dance – and finally the skinwalker falters. The blade of the knife cracks and shivers into a thousand pieces, raining down on Cecil's body and onto the earth. I – the Shaman, the Skinwalker, the Lord of All – drop the broken handle. It clatters away across the floor. I am being forced out of this fine vessel, this body of my dreams.

'Enough, Cecil!' Kit cries. 'I will not kill you. I will not free you from your soul. Far better to let you live.'

Cecil Baker is waking from the trance. He is wobbling on his feet. His face is rigid with terror. The skinwalker is gone.

I, Kit, fall to my knees, half sobbing, half laughing.

I look up at the ruined man. At his cruel, old face.

'Cecil, listen to me,' I say softly. 'I am back.'

Cecil Baker doesn't understand me. His eyes are vacant and glassy; they stare at nothing. A puddle of drool has collected at the corner of his mouth and is starting to dribble down his chin. His hands flop by his side. At any moment he looks as if he might simply collapse. I have an inkling then of what has happened to him. It has been too much. The man has lost his mind. I walk over to him and gently push him down onto the floor. Kneeling, I make sure he is settled. It will do him good to rest.

At this moment, when I know in my bones that Cecil Baker will no longer threaten anyone, I feel no joy. Because for a moment, locked in combat with the skinwalker, I felt, truly felt, what it was like to be that man. Locked in some arid place where you can only take – and never give. Where the only feeling is that of control, of possession. I know now that no punishment I could ever dream up would equal the hell on earth of being Cecil Baker.

Something else has crept into my feelings for this old man. This man who has tormented me, my friends and family so long. I feel sorry for him. Images flash through my mind: Cecil playing on the swings with my nine-year-old mother. A young man in a shabby brown suit, setting out on life with his brother, Cyril. This man was once my mother's friend.

All around us, as I help Cecil to settle on the floor, the *kachinas* are fluttering, unsure what to do. I see one or two creep away, taking advantage of the rain and the shadows. Through the muffled movements and the pelting rain I hear a sharp cry. It is coming from the writhing shapes by that terrible basalt altar.

'Kit, is it you? Please tell me you're back.'

'Yes, Waldo, I am back.'

At that a burst of joy from the others.

'The skinwalker is gone!'

Gently placing Cecil's arms in his lap, I rise and rejoin my friends.

❧ Epilogue ❧

I pen these few words in my little maple-timbered cabin on the SS *Timbuktu*. It is a fine new steamer, which is taking us across the oceans, back to Father, Oxford and afternoon tea with hot buttered scones.

Home: green meadows, the call of larks and the spires of Oxford rising in the early-morning drizzle. How I long for it. It will refresh my spirits, after an adventure which has felt like a waking nightmare. Already, as I leave America behind, I feel uncomplicatedly happy. I am able to talk of gowns with Rachel, discussing whether the lilac crêpe or the maroon organza suits her better. With Waldo I debate the best ways to get rich quick. I can, if my head is particularly strong, even talk about stolen treasure with Aunt Hilda or cathode rays with Isaac – not that Isaac will expect me to do more than look interested and smile.

So here we are – healthy and happy – sailing back home, the place where we know we *belong*. All except Waldo, that is. America has made a huge impression on him. Its energy and size draw him. He says the next century will belong

276

to America. While I am not sure he is right – everyone knows Great Britain's empire is the most important in the world – I admire him for seeking new challenges. Anyway, he plans to return. He has asked me, in a roundabout way, if I could see myself living in California or New York.

To tell the truth, I am feeling a little dizzy, for Waldo has just left my cabin. He held my hand – and for a moment I thought he meant to . . . Well, it doesn't matter, for every time I am with Waldo now I feel guilty. You see, when I was possessed by the skinwalker, when I struck Waldo across the face, I broke his nose. The doctors have reset it. Sadly it remains slightly twisted out of shape. My friend is still the handsomest boy I know. However, it cannot be denied that his nose does look a little odd.

(Is it very, very wrong of me to think that we now make a less ill-matched pair? Yes, it is. I never had such an ungracious thought.)

Luckily Waldo has forgiven me for breaking his nose. I am not sure how long this mood will last. It is in Waldo's nature to be strong, even arrogant, and in mine to argue. I also don't know about living in America. After all, I am only thirteen. I will have plenty of time to decide these things after I return to my father and Downside Towers. Yes, Father is determined to send me to boarding school. For the present, I have had quite enough of adventure and have decided not to fight his plans. Rachel, hopefully, will join me at the school. I will see my other friends in the long holidays.

Now I come to the saddest part of my tale: Cecil Baker. As I had understood in the Grand Canyon, his spirit was broken, his wits well and truly gone. The awful things he had done to his own mind had left him little more than a vegetable. He eats, sleeps and talks like a small child. He is as helpless as a babe. We found a hospital in a little town called Oakglade, in the sunny hills of California. We left Cecil there with his own nurse, under the care of a doctor in horn-rimmed spectacles, but far from anyone who loved him, if such a person still exists after the death of his brother.

When we returned from the Grand Canyon to San Francisco, we had our first glad tidings. The only truly good news to come from all our adventures. It turned out that Cyril Baker had made a will. He left the whole of his vast fortune to . . . us!

This confused me at first, because I believed he'd given most of his money away. Not so, it seemed; there was still a fortune he'd been unwilling to part with. Before you become too excited, imagining us millionaires, breakfasting on ices and bathing in powdered pearls, the money has been left in trust. This means solicitors are to manage the fortune till Rachel and I turn twenty-one. It isn't, however, for us. When we come of age, we will only be trustees, able to give the money to worthy charities.

Yes, that's right. Your friends, Kit Salter and Rachel Ani, will take charge of this whole immense fortune. Waldo, Isaac and Aunt Hilda have not been mentioned in the will. We will be enormously powerful, able to give thousands of pounds to people who need our help. Rachel is already researching where she will spend the money. I know she intends to campaign for an end to all forms of slavery – thus righting some of the Baker brothers' wrongs.

I can see why Cyril Baker entrusted the care of his fortune to Rachel: she is honest to the core and will not try to steal or squander it. I was surprised, at first, that he chose to include me. Then I was handed a note by his lawyers in San Francisco.

Dear Kit,

By the time you read this I will be dead. I do not complain – I deserve my fate. I hope you return from the Grand Canyon with your spirit intact. I am praying for you, even from beyond the funeral pyre.

I leave you my fortune because I believe you will have the generosity of spirit to do with great wealth what I could not. By this I mean thinking of others before yourself. I have faith in you, Kit, to do what you can to make some amends for the wounds I have left behind in this world. Because I know you to be kind and a fighter, but not an absolute angel, I have added Rachel Ani to the trustees of my fortune. It is not that I don't have faith in you, but her clear head will curb your wildest schemes.

My blessings from the beyond,
Cyril Baker

Kind and a fighter but not an absolute angel . . . As I read these lines my eyes welled up with tears. It seems Cyril knew me better than I'd supposed.